Fisherman's Bend

FISHERMAN'S BEND

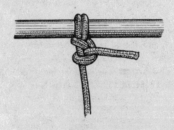

LINDA
GREENLAW

HYPERION

New York

Copyright © 2008 Linda Greenlaw

Library of Congress Cataloging-in-Publication Data
Greenlaw, Linda
  Fisherman's bend / Linda Greenlaw.
       p.   cm.
  ISBN: 978-1-4013-2235-9
  1. Insurance investigators—Fiction   2. Maine —Fiction.   I. Title.
PS3607.R457F57   2008
813'.6—dc22

                                        2008019185

                        Mass Market
                  ISBN: 978-0-7868-8592-3

Hyperion books are available for special promotions and premiums. For details contact the HarperCollins Special Markets Department in the New York office at 212-207-7528, fax 212-207-7222, or email spsales@harpercollins.com.

FIRST MASS MARKET EDITION

10 9 8 7 6 5 4 3 2 1

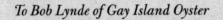

To Bob Lynde of Gay Island Oyster

Fisherman's Bend

1

I STOOD AT THE STERN facing aft and watched the walls of Cobble Harbor gently melt into the rainbow sherbet foliage of Quoddy Head. The Head, high and abrupt, proudly displayed its seasonal colors; a stand of hardwoods stretched up and around the rocky bluff like an Indian headdress. As Cal pushed the throttle up a bit, I sighed with the realization that Mother Nature's ornamentation would soon be gone—like Christmas cards plucked on January 2 from their temporary refrigerator-door home. So this was autumn in New England. I was only a child when, decades ago, my mother moved my brother and me from Acadia Island, which was just across the bay, all the way down to Florida—the most exotic place she could think of. But South Florida's orange groves didn't hold a candle to this, I thought.

The deck swayed beneath me as Cal rounded a buoy, causing me to brace my left leg. The increased speed, a cool comb that parted the hair on the back of my head, was another reminder of things to come. A weathered red navigational buoy, nun number "4," suddenly appeared at the edge of my peripheral vision, and then bobbed its matronly figure in the small swells we had caused.

We sped east across Cobscook Bay and away from Green Haven as the center of our wake seemed to zip back up what the stem had so brazenly exposed. The surface beyond the churning wake was unusually smooth and protective.

I'm Jane Bunker, a newly deputized marine insurance investigator. I moved to Green Haven, Maine, in June of this year to start a new life. The old life? Well, suffice it to say I left it in Miami. It's important to note that my change of scene was nothing like the proverbial heart left in San Francisco. If my move north were a song, it would be a slightly happier tune—no regrets. Well, almost none. Dropping my position as chief detective of Miami-Dade County in favor of that of a lowly insurance investigator was a quick, albeit calculated, descent on the career ladder. Though, since my return to Maine, I had succeeded in pulling myself up a rung, and had just picked up the title assistant deputy of Knox County. Like many of my neighbors, I now wore more than one hat. Deputy sheriff was a part-time, need-based employment. It was simple supply and demand; little criminal activity meant little need for my deputy services.

The deputy gig, still in its infancy (not unlike the marine consulting, which was also relatively new to me), was the result of a lack of interest on behalf of local law enforcement in venturing out to the remote extremities that comprised the territories I cover in my chief job of insurance gal. In this respect I was now able to kill two birds. I could survey damaged property, investigate crime scenes, and write corresponding reports. (Although math is not my strength, I do realize that according to that list, any stones I cast may take care of three birds.)

My boss at Eastern Marine Safety Consultants, Mr. Dubois, had telephoned at nine o'clock this morning with an assignment to inspect damage to some of *Quest*'s deck equipment. He said that *Quest* was a privately owned research vessel authorized by the State of Maine to survey a piece of ocean floor in Cobscook Bay. A large aquaculture outfit, North Atlantic Shell Farms, had applied to lease this particular bottom from the state with ambitions of growing oysters. Surveying the bottom was part of the application process. According to Mr. Dubois, someone had maliciously vandalized some of the deck equipment aboard the vessel. In his opinion, "some of those interbreds with too much time on their hands" had thought of this as entertainment. "Just a quick inspection, a few pictures, and a report will be fine. This is a very important customer for the insurance company. Don't get too . . . well, you know," he advised.

"Thorough?"

"Look, Jane. They don't want to press any charges. They just want to collect what's coming to them, get their equipment repaired, do their job, and get out of that chromosome deficiency zone."

"Come on. Cobble Harbor can't be that bad," I said hopefully.

"Well, it's just . . . remote."

"Worse than Green Haven?" I asked. My new hometown felt like the end of the Earth to me. After our conversation and a look at the road map, I had called Cal. To avoid accusations of double-dipping, I hired Cal to transport me to and from Cobble Harbor via his boat, *Sea Pigeon.* I offered to pay Cal the same $20 per hour that I would receive from the County Sheriff's Department for my time. Cal was happy to oblige. The pay was a bit more than he had been getting at Turners' Fish Plant before it burned to the ground, and this was an opportunity for him to get back on the water, where he had spent the majority of his working life. Sure, I could have driven my car from Green Haven to Cobble Harbor. But driving the length of the two peninsulas I would have needed to traverse would have consumed the majority of my day, not to mention a significant portion of what life remained in my 1987 Plymouth Duster. By water the distance was a very manageable seventeen miles. Economics aside, I thought a boat ride would be nice.

A chronic early bird, I had arrived at our prearranged meeting spot a full twenty minutes ahead of our scheduled rendezvous of 11:30 A.M. And I learned that Cal Dunham was even twitchier than I am when I found him already aboard *Sea Pigeon* at the public landing behind Bartlett's Store. Cal is in his early seventies, tall, but stooped from a long career as an offshore fisherman. He is a man of few words, with the wide honest face of a New Englander. After the unpleasant events following the murder of the town drunk six months ago, Cal had proven himself a steady friend. *Sea Pigeon* was tied to the dock with her engine idling smoothly. I stepped aboard, Cal untied and coiled the single dock line, and off we went toward Quoddy Head.

And I was right to think a boat ride would be nice. It *was* nice—lovely, actually. We arrived at the town dock in Cobble Harbor, as Cal said we would, at just a few minutes past noon. The *Sea Pigeon* seemed diminished in size by the looming stern of *Quest*. The larger vessel cast a square shadow into which we crept as two men appeared on the wharf to catch our dock lines. To some observers, the small mound between Cal's shoulders indicated a degree of decrepitude. But his boat-handling skills, agility, and no-nonsense demeanor revealed competence of a level that thrust helping hands back to pockets as the old man secured his boat and nodded an okay for me to step ashore. My promise to be quick was met with a smile and, "Take your time. I ain't goin' nowhere."

. The long step up from *Sea Pigeon* to the dock was made easier by a large hand extended by the taller of the two men standing on the dock. The men seemed to have been waiting for me. Before the tall man released his grip, introductions were made. "You must be Jane Bunker. I'm Dane Stevens, captain of *Quest*." Black sideburns spilled from beneath a red baseball cap sporting the ship's logo, which matched the embroidered patch on the breast of his light gray sweatshirt. His dungarees appeared to have been starched with perfect creases that ended just above comfortable-looking Sperry Top-Siders. "This is our chief archaeologist, Quentin Molnar—otherwise known as Quasar." The utterance of the nickname was delivered with a broad, white smile that confirmed that this was indeed a friendly mission. The ever important first impression was a positive one; confident and competent, Dane Stevens seemed captainly.

Quasar, on the other hand, was ill at ease. Perhaps he was one of those scientists whom you suspect is more at home in a laboratory than out in the world of human beings; Quentin Molnar squinted nervously behind thick glasses and shifted his weight from foot to foot as he spoke. "Ms. Bunker, thank you. Thanks. Ahh, thanks for coming so quickly. We appreciate your coming here. We're really very grateful. So, thank you." Quasar was absolutely disheveled. The tails of his white oxford shirt were half in and half out of severely wrinkled khakis. It was clear which side he slept on as his thick mop of reddish hair was so lopsided I fought the urge to tilt my head while he was speaking. "We were scheduled to begin work today and now vandals have really screwed us up. We've been vandalized. Vandals have screwed up our schedule." I wondered if Quasar always repeated himself, or if I was making him nervous. "I've already ordered replacement parts for what I can't fix. I can fix a lot of it. I had to order a few things, but not too much. I hope FedEx can find this place. Do you know if FedEx delivers here?"

"I don't know. I'm here to inspect the damage, send pictures and a claim to the boat's insurance company, and file a police report. Shall we go aboard and have a look?" I asked.

"Oh, yes, of course. Yes, come. Follow me. We'll go aboard. Right this way," Quasar said as he turned and scurried toward the aluminum gangplank that connected the top of the dock to *Quest*. He shuffled across the metal pathway and hopped down onto the deck without a glance back to see if I was with him. The handsome captain motioned for me to go ahead of him with a shrug and a half smile that I took as an apology for Quasar's manners and awkwardness. Soon the three of us stood in the middle of a basketball court–sized work area surrounded by cranes, dredges, winches, a submersible, and several pieces of equipment I didn't recognize. Dane Stevens excused himself to complete some unfinished project, the details of which I don't recall. Slightly disappointed to be left alone with the nerdy archaeologist, I sighed—story of my life.

I quickly got down to the job at hand, anxious to attempt to please my boss by doing only the bare minimum, even though that was against my nature. Quasar, who became articulate on his home turf, led me around the deck in a very educational guided tour of *Quest*'s special equipment. He described in some detail the workings of the magnetoscope and the galeazzi lance, both of which appeared to have been beaten with a sledgehammer. He explained that the magnetoscope was used to detect ferrous masses on the ocean floor and the lance was designed to remove sediment buildup around any potential historical sites. "Historical sites? What kind of historical sites?" I asked as I zoomed my camera in on a circuit board that was exposed and smashed. "I assumed that you'd be surveying to see if the area is suitable for aquaculture." I turned to Quasar to see what he'd say, but I was just being polite. Sure, I was curious to learn more.

But I needed only a few pictures and an official report, not commentary or opinion.

"Oh, we are indeed. That's why we're here; to check the proposed site for the oyster farmers. But in Cobscook Bay we're thinking we might find remnants of Native American campsites. Federal and state laws require off-shore projects to hire archaeological companies to determine whether activity will harm historically significant remains." Quasar pushed his eyeglasses onto the bridge of his nose. "We're also checking water quality, tidal flow, and other factors and elements that make the area conducive to growing oysters. That's all North Atlantic wants to know. They want to be assured that the site they are applying for to lease from the State of Maine is ripe for their purposes. They aren't concerned about anything else."

"Indians camped offshore?" I asked, immediately forming a negative opinion of money spent on such foolishness.

"Sure," Quasar said, a smile on his face. "During the last ice age the level of the ocean plummeted over three hundred feet. But then the glaciers melted, the sea level rose again and drowned what we hope to find—intact underwater cultural sites. How did the first humans get to this continent? Land bridge from Siberia to Alaska following big game?" Quasar's eyes widened with impassioned energy and seemed to grow tenfold with the help of the thick lenses framed in black plastic rims. "Or was it via the coastal route from Europe? It's a debate that could be settled by finding submerged settlements with evidence of tools or food gathering." Quasar's voice had gone up a full octave. By the time Quasar had completely saturated me with his passion for archaeological expeditions, I knew that he'd only scratched the surface of his vast knowledge. Through his work he intended to support theories of whys and wheres of the earliest inhabitants of New England. Although I had all I needed to get the ball rolling toward reimbursement from *Quest*'s insurance company for all damages, I asked a few questions—more out of curiosity than anything else. I wasn't feigning interest out of politeness anymore. I was genuinely intrigued.

It was abundantly clear that Quasar's connection to aquaculture was due only to the fact that North Atlantic Shell Farms was footing the bill to allow Quasar and what I assumed would be a team of scientists the opportunity to delve below. And it was also clear that this wild-eyed archaeologist was hoping to find exactly what his employers didn't want him to discover. A historic site would definitely be a setback for a company that would prosper in establishing oyster beds on the ocean floor. As a point of interest, Quasar mentioned that the vandals had sabotaged only what was needed for underwater exploration. None of the vessel's propulsion, electronic navigational aids, or other state-of-the-art systems had been disturbed in any way. To his eye, in contrast to what my boss thought about a random strike born of boredom and stupidity, this incident was a direct attack targeting the archaeological aspect of the survey. Quasar was agitated in a way that I found consistent with any victim of a personal attack.

Now Quasar had piqued my interest. I knew that I wasn't supposed to bother with motive, but I couldn't stop myself from asking, "Who would care?" And when I saw his face fall in utter dejection, I quickly added, "I mean, who would want to keep you from doing such important work?" Quasar attempted to drag a freckled, bony hand through his tangled mess of red curls, but found the spiderweb of hair too embroiled to traverse. As he tried to pull his fingers from where they were caught, deep in his rat's nest, he shared his opinions and theories as though he'd been hypothesizing for some time. A lot of criminal investigating is timing. And knowing when to ask the right question is my forte. While Quasar was in the midst of a very long-winded answer to my query, I decided that it was a good thing there would be no charges pressed, as the list of possible suspects was, in Quasar's opinion, quite lengthy. Quasar was acutely aware of the many factions who had vested interests in Cobscook Bay and he led me through his understanding of the situation as we moved slowly in the direction of my ride home.

Quasar thought the damage could have been done by any member of two large, extended families of lobster fishermen who worked on Cobscook Bay, the Alleys and the Beals. It seemed that, like the legendary Hatfields and McCoys, these two families had been feuding for nearly a century. So many generations into the fight, no one remembered exactly what had caused the rift. But everyone knew that a battle was presently being waged in Cobscook Bay, and it was all in the name of lobster. According to the scientist, this was the gear war that had escalated to exceed all gear wars. This controversy had gone beyond the occasional molesting of the other side's fishing gear—lobster traps, in this case. Quasar, who had been in Cobble Harbor for only a few days, had learned of beatings, burnings, and sinkings. "A reasonable person might speculate that a threat from a third party like North Atlantic Shell Farms might cause the Alleys and Beals to join forces against their common enemy. Their sheer strength in numbers could make aquaculture impossible here if they banded together and went about defeating the project legally. But these aren't reasonable people. So it could have been either family, or both, or neither." Quasar ran a hand along the badly battered metal housing of the magnetoscope as if caressing a wound.

"And then there's the Native Americans," Quasar continued. "Both the Passamaquoddy and Maliseet tribes claim to have aboriginal rights to fish Cobscook Bay unencumbered by state or federal rules. Once the lobster traps come ashore, the Indians move into the bay to harvest sea urchins."

"Wouldn't the Native Americans encourage your research if they felt the results would protect some . . . Well, if they believed there could be evidence of . . ." I struggled with the politically correct terminology.

"Heck no!" Quasar rescued me. "Nothing is sacred to anyone other than to the very oldest members of either tribe. There are no jobs in this area. The Native Americans are split on the aquaculture issue. The enormous scope of this aquaculture might infringe on a lot of the grounds claimed by ancestral fishing rights, but would provide some decent jobs, too."

"Hatfields, McCoys, Passamaquoddy, Maliseet . . . Anyone else?" I was once again grateful not to have to get to the bottom of this one.

"I guess the major oil companies would be inconvenienced by having to reroute ships. Many tankers use Cobscook Bay as a shipping channel in their deliveries up the river." I wondered why this possibility was secondary to feuding fishermen and disenfranchised Indians. "And, like anything else, there are always a number of citizens who just don't like change," Quasar said with a degree of resignation in his voice. I understood his tone as a cue to wish him luck before hopping back aboard *Sea Pigeon*.

On my way out, I poked my head through the fo'c'sle door hoping to find the captain, but didn't. Rather than wandering around the ship, I asked Quasar to please relay my thanks to his captain. Relieved that my request was not met with a knowing look from the nerdy man, I realized that he must be accustomed to his friend getting all the attention from women. And I understood that I would not become one of those women, as the handsome one did not appear for even a distant wave goodbye as Cal and I left the dock for the outer harbor. Oh well, I thought, I probably wouldn't return to Cobble Harbor for a long time, and the chances of running into Dane Stevens in my landlocked travels were slim.

I turned away from the *Quest* and joined Cal at the helm, where he navigated a twisted path heavily studded with the multicolored bullet floats that marked lobster traps. Buoys bowed and curtsied as they were swept aside by the water cleaved at the bow. Cal piloted and I talked. I told him about what I'd found on the *Quest* and what I'd learned from Quasar, leaving no opportunity for my hired water chauffeur to reply or comment. I talked knowing that Cal was less than a sounding board, as I'd learned that he seldom gives any indication of what he's absorbing and what he's deflecting. Cal's concentration seemed to be split between the cigarette he was enjoying and the avoidance of lobster gear while maintaining a westward course. So my talking became more like thinking aloud in the presence of someone barely paying attention.

A white speck on the horizon was the only evidence of anyone working in this hotly contested area of Cobscook Bay. This late in the afternoon, I imagined that all of the other lobster fishermen had given up work for the day. I took comfort in the solitude while rehashing facts and formulating theories. I'm often considered the queen of "mountains from molehills," I know. But I'm right at least some of the time. When I stumbled across the town drunk's body on the shore back in June, everyone else thought his death had just been an accident, but I thought there was more to it than that. After a couple instances of insurance fraud, an act of arson that took out Green Haven's primary employer, and several attempts on my life, it turned out I was right. Since then, things have been a little on the dull side.

The white speck on the horizon gradually took shape: a lone lobster boat circling around and around.

At our present speed I had assumed we would arrive back in Green Haven before dark. That meant I would have time to get home to my apartment, transcribe to-day's work into the computer, and send my completed report along to the insurance company. That was one nice thing about my new career, I thought. Most of the time, I could complete an assignment in one day. It was great to have such a sense of accomplishment and be able to measure success in a quantitative way each evening and wake up the following morning with a whole new perspective. Very seldom does anything linger. I was already wondering what tomorrow would bring. This work was less than exciting, but hell, hadn't I had my fill of excitement in Miami? I hoped that I would be able to hire Cal in the future. I wondered whether he'd be interested in driving me to assignments via land. Maybe I would ask him. Suddenly my thoughts were interrupted by the slowing of the *Sea Pigeon*'s engine.

I turned to face forward again and noticed that we were getting fairly close to the lobster boat I had seen on the horizon. The clean, white boat was in the perpetual, lazy, starboard circle identical to that of any boat hauling lobster traps. Cal slowed the engine down to an idle as we approached the boat, whose bow now bent away from ours. Maybe Cal knew this boat or was a friend of its captain, I thought. I wouldn't be surprised if Cal knew everyone on the bay. He'd certainly spent enough time out here in the past. Now the port side faced us as Cal threw the *Sea Pigeon*'s engine out of gear. Oh, I thought, wouldn't it be nice to surprise my landlords with lobster for dinner? I wondered how much cash I had in my pocket. Now the stern came gracefully into view—*Eva B.* Beautiful boat, I thought. And a pretty name. I wondered if the "B" stood for Beal. I felt some paper money in my pocket and figured I had enough for three lobsters as long as they weren't too big. I glanced at Cal. His face was ashen. "What?" I asked.

Cal swallowed hard and never took his eyes off the *Eva B.* I looked over the bow and directly into the cockpit of the lobster boat. A numbing of my limbs and sickness in my gut grew stronger as Cal confirmed what I saw.

"There's no one aboard her."

2

THE ABSENCE OF LIFE aboard the *Eva B.* evoked a dark image that quickly overshadowed my other thoughts and doused my hunger for lobster. The scene was numbing in what it suggested. An abandoned boat running in a dizzying and endless loop was something I had heard about during my years working the coast of South Florida. But until now, I had never personally encountered one. Floridian stone crabbers and bandit fishermen who worked inshore would cut expenses in times of slow harvests by laying off deckhands and fishing single-handedly. Maine lobstermen often did the same. Of all their expenses—bait, fuel, gear, etc.—help was the only one a captain could leave at the dock and still be able to produce. Although fishing alone was generally considered to be unwise to the point of foolhardy, a lot of small-boat operators did it; many claimed to prefer solitude at sea. By the looks of what was unfolding in front of me, this was also the case in Cobscook Bay.

Cal pulled the throttle back to an idle as we watched the *Eva B.* complete another full circle. I prayed, as I knew Cal did, that a baseball-capped head would suddenly appear in the small rectangular doorway that led to the cutty cabin between the helm bulkhead and stem.

"Maybe someone's down forward," I suggested, verbalizing our shared hope.

"It's possible," Cal said as he brushed by me and opened the half-size door that led to the small triangular storage area of our boat's cabin. Cal stepped down into the fiberglass cave, vanished into relative darkness, and then reappeared with an air horn in one hand and a rusty shotgun in the other. Cal placed the gun in the corner formed by the meeting of bulkhead and gunwale, setting its butt on the deck firmly. In answer to what I suppose was a surprised look from me, Cal stated that he never boarded another man's vessel unannounced or uninvited. "Consider this my announcement," he said as he placed the air horn on the dash, reengaged the transmission, and maneuvered to draw us nearer the *Eva B*.

"Is that thing loaded?" I asked, not yet sure whether the presence of a firearm made me feel more or less anxious.

"Should be," Cal said, grabbing the horn and giving the can of compressed air a brisk shake. "I ain't used it since the Blessing of the Fleet—Fourth of July." I understood that Cal knew full well that my question had not been in regard to the horn, so I assumed the shotgun was loaded. Of course it was, I thought. What good was an empty gun?

As we passed the *Eva B*.'s stern, Cal pressed the red plastic button, releasing a long whistle of air from the can through the six-inch, trumpet-shaped, polished aluminum horn, resulting in a very impressive ear-splitting blast. He removed his index finger from the button, cutting the blaring noise like a meat cleaver would a wet noodle. We waited and watched for several anxious seconds for a startled and embarrassed captain to scramble out and into view, perhaps waving a wrench to signal he was okay and thanking us for our concern. But no one showed. Cal gave the horn a couple of short squirts, the volume of each of which made me flinch. Sadly, my flinching was the only reaction to Cal's "announcement."

"One of us has to go aboard her," Cal said.

"I'll go," I said without hesitation, and moved behind Cal to the starboard gunwale. Of the two of us, I knew I was more able physically to perform the boat hop if calisthenics should be required. Cal nodded his consent and turned his attention to driving the *Sea Pigeon*. I briefly wondered what the temperature of the water was. I'd always heard that, all things considered, death from hypothermia wasn't a bad way to go.

As the gap narrowed between the *Sea Pigeon* and the *Eva B.*, Cal gave me last-minute instructions over his right shoulder. "Don't climb onto the rail until we're ahead of her wake. And don't jump. I'll put you right alongside her. Just knock her out of gear, and we'll raft up." The *Eva B.* had been circling long enough to have built up quite a confused chop all around her. Death as a result of being crushed between the boats would be on the more unpleasant end of the scale. And to think that just a few minutes ago this day offered nothing more than a routine inspection of vandalized equipment aboard a research vessel. Cal increased the throttle and brought the *Sea Pigeon*'s starboard bow against the *Eva B.*'s port

beam just aft of her house. Both boats were bouncing
enough to make the transfer hairy. I climbed onto the rail
and grabbed the edge of the overhead for stability. The
few seconds that passed as I waited for Cal to close the
V-shaped opening between the rails were filled not with
fear, but with a classic clip from an old Western racing
through my mind. Cowboy movies always had a scene
like this with our hero jumping from one horse to another, I thought. The movie in my head was interrupted
when Cal yelled, "Now!"

At this instant, the boats were pressed together from
beam to stern. The step I made was an easy one; rail to
rail. I released my grip from the *Sea Pigeon*'s roof and
hopped down into the cockpit of the *Eva B.* Once both of
my feet were planted safely on deck, Cal peeled away to
port, signaling a reminder for me to pull the *Eva B.*'s gear
shift into the neutral position. I hustled to the helm, eased
the throttle control back to an idle, and jerked the gear
shift toward me so it was vertical. With her engine disen-
gaged, the *Eva B.* slowed from a hearty jog to a peaceful
drift as the waves created by the two wakes moved away
in circles of growing circumference and shrinking height.
Cal was now about a hundred feet off my starboard side.
He tied fenders at *Sea Pigeon*'s stern and midship in preparation for securing to the *Eva B.*, or "rafting up" as he
had said. I kept my attention focused on the old man and
my back purposefully to the door that led to the only
compartment of the *Eva B.* that was unexposed. I couldn't
help but think that compartment was large enough to
hold a person. Yes, I was anxious.

Cal was lucky I am so comfortable on boats. Much of my childhood leisure time was spent crawling around the commercial docks of Miami—crawling, like a wharf rat. I was like the proverbial bad penny in my persistence against the advice and even scolding I received from nearly everyone I encountered. Merchant seamen, longshoremen, fishermen, sailors . . . Men of the sea in general all advised me to stay away. It took a while, but I was eventually able to convince all concerned that I was safer on the waterfront than I was on the city streets. Or at least I was *as* safe. When ships' cooks started slipping me treats and deckhands shared trinkets and stories in broken English of faraway ports, I knew I was in. But it wasn't until I won over Archie that I really belonged to this salty extended family.

Archie, a lifelong commercial fisherman whom I now considered my best friend and mentor, gave me my most cherished gift—an education in all things related to the sea. In return, Archie got cheap labor. Cal reminded me of Archie, which explained my immediate fondness and trust in him. Of course, I had never explained my boat savvy to Cal. I didn't need to. On the water, ability is displayed in action and reaction. Words don't cut it. So, when Cal eased the *Sea Pigeon* alongside *Eva B.*, he didn't tell me when or how to take a couple of wraps of a line around a cleat. I just did it.

Now that we were rafted up and drifting in the slight southwesterly breeze, I imagined we looked like an awkward catamaran. "What next?" I asked, as Cal sat on the rail of his boat, shotgun in hand, and slung a leg over the rail and into the *Eva B.*'s cockpit.

Once aboard, Cal smoothed his clothes with a sweep of an open palm and then patted a loose strand of white hair back into place. Cal was always neatly groomed. "We should check down forward before calling the Coast Guard."

"Check for what? Bodies?"

"Well, I don't know about you. But I'd be embarrassed if the Coasties came all the way from Southwest Harbor to find a tired old fisherman down there taking a nap." Cal motioned at the door in the bulkhead with the barrel of his gun, indicating to me that he expected ladies to go first. "You're the deputy." I knew as well as Cal did that if anyone *was* aboard the *Eva B.*, they were not likely to wake up from their "nap."

I approached the door with the apprehension of someone turning the crank on the side of a jack-in-the-box. The pounding in my chest was strangely comforting and exhilarating. I took one last look at Cal's decrepit weapon. I thought about how far a cry this was from the Homeland Security boardings I had been part of off the coast of Key West. Overcoming fear in the face of danger was perhaps the only aspect of my former life that I missed. I took a deep breath and willed myself to be brave the way I always had; then I threw the door open with a bang. The setting sun spilled enough light into the small cabin for me to see that all it contained were spare coils of line, buoys, buckets of oil, belts, hoses, life jackets, and cleaning supplies. "See?" I said, standing to the side of the doorway so that Cal could look, too. "Nobody home. Let's call the Coast Guard."

Cal was already straddling the crease between the boats when I turned to discuss our course of action. I followed him back over the gunwales, feeling more at ease aboard the *Sea Pigeon*. The likelihood that a man had been lost at sea from the deck of the *Eva B.* gave the boat a certain shiver factor; a creepy aura difficult to ignore. Cal hailed the Coast Guard on channel 16 of his VHF radio, switched to a working frequency at their request, and relayed our predicament. As a rule (and this episode was no exception), government agencies have strict protocols from which they will not stray—no matter how ridiculous. Like the silly frequency-switching business. I was relieved that Cal was manning the radio. While the Coast Guard dispatcher ran Cal through the usual hoops of seemingly unrelated questions, I scanned the horizon and considered different scenarios of varying plausibility.

Weather, it seemed to me, could not have been a contributing factor to the situation we had happened upon. "Are you in any immediate danger, Captain?" I detected an accent—not local—in the voice of the young Coast Guardsman I now heard over the radio. Cal gave the lowdown again, quickly and with more urgency this time. Although it wasn't impossible that a freak sea or rogue wave had swept the *Eva B.*'s captain overboard, I thought it was highly unlikely. "How many persons are onboard the vessel, Captain?" Neither Cal nor I knew which vessel the dispatcher was asking about. I suspected that he didn't either. "How many persons are onboard *your* vessel, Captain?" Yes, an accent, I thought—definitely Midwestern.

Falling overboard while taking a leak was a risk, I supposed. I had heard and had stored in my memory that when lost bodies were recovered from the ocean, a high percentage of the victims' flies were open. "Are you taking on water at this time, Captain? Captain, we request that you don your personal flotation devices at this time." Cal was getting annoyed with the boy from Kansas with whom he was trying to communicate. I was amused when the veteran mariner lied by assuring the Coastie that we had indeed donned our life jackets. Cal asked again when we could expect a Coast Guard vessel to arrive on the scene and suggested that an aircraft be deployed to begin a search of the vicinity.

Cal tried valiantly to explain the situation again—that we weren't in any danger, but a man was missing at sea. I continued to ponder what might have happened. It didn't seem possible that a man of average height could accidentally fall overboard from the *Eva B*. The gunwales along the length of her work space were high enough to meet anyone at mid-thigh. No, I couldn't see an accidental falling overboard, fly down or not. The missing fisherman most probably had been dragged over the side or stern by his own lobster gear. It wasn't unusual for rescuers to recover a drowned fisherman by hauling his gear and finding the corpse entangled in the line. Judging from the size and number of masonry bricks built into the lobster traps I'd seen all over Green Haven, Mark Spitz himself wouldn't have been able to stay on the surface if he were attached to one as it dove for the bottom. "Roger, Captain. Please relay your present position in lat/long. Over."

Cal looked at me and shook his head, raising his hands in surrender before keying the radio's microphone for what I believed would be his last transmission: "Our present position is approximately ten feet northeast of our last position given to you at precisely sixteen hundred hours. Is there a boat under way? Has a plane been deployed? There may be a man treading water out here, damn it! Over."

"Roger, Captain. Stand by."

Cal left the microphone dangling from its cord from the overhead and joined me where I sat, resting on the starboard rail. A freshly lit cigarette soothed what the inexperienced Coast Guardsman and red tape had rubbed the wrong way. While Cal smoked, I pulled a pad from my tote bag and jotted some notes, including our latitude and longitude, which were displayed in large black digits on the face of the GPS. "Not you, too," Cal said, lightly enough to be interpreted as a tease.

"I just thought it would be wise to calculate our drift," I answered without taking my eyes off the screen. "It might help narrow the field for the search."

"Point six knots to the northeast." I should have known Cal would be ahead of me in this game, but continued to go through the motions of calculating. I knew it might be quite some time before the Coast Guard arrived and took the *Eva B.* off our hands, so I climbed back aboard her and looked around more closely than I had initially. I started below in the cabin, where I saw nothing out of the ordinary except for an abundance of shipping supplies. It was like a little warehouse. There was a stack of cardboard boxes printed with LIVE LOBSTERS— HANDLE WITH CARE, a tape gun and a folder with pre-printed shipping labels. The return address on the labels read COBSCOOK LOBSTER COMPANY, which did nothing to help ID the missing fisherman. Everything else in storage was either for maintenance and repair, or they were the usual supplies one would find aboard any lobster boat, such as lobster bands, spare banding tools, a lobster measure, a short gaff, and half a dozen blue cotton work gloves. The gloves were size large. So for all of my poking around, the size of his hands was all I learned of the missing fisherman.

Two steps up and out of the cabin I was back beside the helm. I removed the top of a small cooler, ignoring Cal's comment about the man's lunch. The cooler was filled with frozen gel packs, so it seemed obvious that the man had intended to box his catch aboard and ship the boxes as soon as he got back to port.

The color sounder mounted on the dash showed the ocean floor beneath us in a medium red horizontal line; yellow numbers illuminated the depth at twelve fathoms. In over seventy feet of water, the missing fisherman had certainly not walked home. A GPS track plotter displayed an array of colorful event marks that I assumed represented exact locations of the lobster traps. A lime green track like an endless doodle ran across the monitor in curlicues that terminated at the white blinking boat-shaped symbol; this showed our position in relation to traps and landmass. I found the button that controlled the scale of the picture on the monitor, and zoomed out until I found the far end of the corkscrewed wake. Somewhat of an electronics geek, I admired the top-of-the-line equipment aboard the *Eva B.*

"Wow," I said as I roughly estimated the time and distance the *Eva B.* had traveled since wandering off the well-beaten, lime green track. "We're more than three miles northeast of where it appears the boat strayed from the line of traps he was fishing. At point six knots, that's way too long to hope for a miracle. No one can hold their breath that long."

"Where's the goddamned plane?" Cal stood, shielded his eyes with a hand, and searched the sky. "It'll be pitch-black here in three hours. There'll be no chance to save him if he has to wait until morning."

"But a plane won't help much if he's on the bottom tangled in his own gear," I added.

"He ain't."

"Ain't what?"

"Ain't snarled in his own gear. He wasn't hauling traps. The bottom in this part of the bay is all mud. Look at that boat," Cal said and motioned toward the *Eva B.* "She's clean as a whistle. If he had just hauled and set, there'd be a mess along the rail. And where's the bait? Everything's all tucked away nice and neat. I'd bet he went overboard cleaning her up. Most fellas put the boat in a hard circle while they tidy up after hauling, and most fellas dip a five-gallon bucket over the side for wash-down water. Maybe he lost his balance and got pulled over by the bucket. There're lobsters in the tank, so we know he *had* been hauling. But . . ." Cal stopped his rant and cocked his head to one side. Squinting toward the east he said, "Boats."

Sure enough, there were boats coming from the east. They were approaching quickly, and as they cut the distance I counted eleven. Soon the lead boat, *Ardency,* was rafting to our free side. The two men aboard *Ardency* were dressed in dark orange Grundéns, the waterproof bib overalls worn by most Green Haven fishermen. Almond-shaped black eyes peered from under visors salt-stained from adjusting with wet gloves. The captain, who appeared to be the father of the man in the stern, wasted no time with questions or small talk. He was crossing our deck before his son finished securing the stern line and then hopped from us onto the *Eva B.* Both men were slight of stature, yet had forearms beneath rolled-up flannel sleeves that looked hard enough to drive spikes. What I guessed was half of the Cobble Harbor fleet—either the Hatfields or the McCoys—soon coasted to relative stops all around us. With the circling of wagons came the odd comfort of knowing that Cal and I were not in this probable tragedy alone.

Each of the ten boats on the perimeter was manned in twos by fishermen who stood with arms crossed at chests and stared, waiting for direction. As the seconds ticked by, the younger men began to fidget a bit with what I took as anxiety and disbelief while the more weathered members of the group were stilled by a common resolve that I understood as maturity in the face of almost certainly bad news about the fate of a fellow fraternity member. I wanted to know the missing man's name and ask his age, but it seemed I would have to wait to read it in the newspaper. The man who had jumped aboard the *Eva B.* grabbed the VHF mic and began organizing what I thought would be a search party, but sounded more like a cleanup crew. No one had said a word to either Cal or me.

"All right, boys," he began in a voice deeper than what I imagined his thin frame would produce. "If we each haul between fifty and sixty traps, we can get the bulk of them to the harbor before dark. Keep the gear aboard until I find out what Lillian wants done with it. Let's all meet at the dock tomorrow after the funeral." Funeral! Tomorrow! This was too bizarre, I thought. They hadn't even *looked* for a body. How could they possibly have a service so soon? I glanced at Cal, who shot me a look that had "shut up" all over it. The muscle at the jaw on the side of the captain's face worked in and out as he gave each boat instructions over the radio while he stared at the plotter. "Greg, southeast part of Forsaken Ground. Dan, you take the stuff on Three Fathoms. Phil, looks like there's a full load along the twenty-six line between the Tetons. . . ." And he continued until all ten boats had steamed off. Placing the microphone back into its bracket, he began shutting off all of the *Eva B.*'s electronics and then turned the key to kill the engine.

On his way back across the *Sea Pigeon,* the captain stopped, shook Cal's hand solemnly, and nodded to me. "We heard you call the Coast Guard and came out as fast as we could. Most of us were just getting in from hauling, so we were still aboard our boats. I can't thank you enough. I guess the Coast Guard expects you to stand by with his boat until they get here to tow her in. I have to hustle along now to get a load of his traps before dark. Thanks again." And with that, the man joined his son back aboard *Ardency* and began casting off the lines.

"Shouldn't some of you be searching for him?" I asked as politely as I could. "I mean, what if he's still alive and waiting for someone to pick him out of the water?"

"With all due respect, ma'am, he's not." Both men pushed against the side of *Sea Pigeon* to separate the two boats.

"How do you know?" I asked.

"He can't swim."

"Maybe he's wearing a life jacket." My voice was louder now to cover the growing distance and two diesel engines.

"He never did."

"What if he's clinging to a buoy or piece of driftwood?" I insisted.

"He wouldn't." His hand reached for the gear shift.

"Wouldn't? Why wouldn't he?" I pleaded. "You seem to know him quite well."

"I knew him quite well. He was my brother, Parker Alley."

3

ALTHOUGH IT SEEMED TO take forever, I'm certain that the Coast Guard vessel was in sight within an hour of the *Ardency*'s casting off. *Vigilance,* a large and stately-looking ship with her telltale Coast Guard stripe—a wide red slash on either side of the bow—seemed overkill for the task at hand. As she drew near enough for Cal and me to read the name on her bow, the man on the radio finally gave up his futile attempts to hail the *Sea Pigeon*. I didn't question Cal's ignoring the many calls from the Coast Guard ship, as it was clearly getting closer with each transmission. I had learned long ago how captains feel about unsolicited input from subordinates.

Men in blue uniforms scrambled to place fat bumpers along the ship's hull and flaked lines hand over hand onto the deck, resulting in neat coils ready to heave. A man on the open flybridge called down at us through a megaphone as they drifted at a fifty-foot distance by our starboard beam. "We are preparing to come alongside, Captain."

Cal flashed a thumbs-up toward the megaphone and said softly, "I can see that, dumbass."

There was a little more scrambling before the captain finally engaged the engines and began an awkward maneuvering; first away from us, then back toward us. As it looked like *Vigilance* was coming in for a landing, the man with the megaphone ordered us to stand away from the rail they were now quickly approaching. Cal moved to the helm, where he grasped the wheel with both hands and advised me calmly, "Brace yourself." I did as I was told, joining Cal at the helm and holding on to the edge of the dash tightly. The first attempt by the Coast Guard to come alongside was a glancing blow that caused *Sea Pigeon* and *Eva B.* to career against the inflated rubber fenders between them, designed and intended for this purpose. The cooler fell from the *Eva B.*'s engine hatch with a loud crash, sending frozen gel packs skittering on the deck. No damage. As the Coast Guard ship pulled away for another try I could hear the usual noise from the bridge to the men on deck, not really blaming them for the miss, but indicating to anyone within hearing range that it was because something had not been executed properly that the captain was not able to stick the landing. His second approach was much slower. The ship eased into our starboard rail, and two young men hopped aboard and secured lines.

The next thirty minutes or so were painful. Cal relayed all of the information he had about what had transpired prior to the Coast Guard's arrival on the scene, while an electronics expert examined the *Eva B.*'s plotter, finally coming to the conclusion that the missing fisherman must have fallen overboard. The men were dressed in dark blue jumpsuits and orange life vests from which dangled whistles and safety strobe lights. Each man sported a holstered firearm. The legs of their pants were tucked into black lace-up combat-style boots. It appeared to me that the Coast Guard was currently better suited to respond to breaches of Homeland Security than search and rescue. The Coasties were young and polite and appeared to be embarrassed by their own inexperience. I was relieved that Cal took it easy on them when they asked their silly questions. They had protocol, checklists, and superior officers. It was understood that the young men were doing their jobs as they had been trained. They showed Cal all the respect due to an ancient mariner. Unsure of my jurisdiction as deputy sheriff, I didn't volunteer any information, which I imagined pleased Cal as he began to fidget with impatience. The crew of *Vigilance* was either unwilling to make a decision or unable to move without permission from higher-ups, something they were finally given reluctantly over the VHF radio after what I perceived as an ungodly amount of time between requests.

At last, the captain of the ship was told to take the *Eva B.* in tow, and he quickly ordered his men to do so. When I asked, I was told that they would tow the small boat to their home port and Coast Guard base in Southwest Harbor, where they would investigate and notify family. Neither Cal nor I mentioned that the family needn't be notified. The captain thanked us for being good Samaritans and gave us permission to get under way. When Cal made a move toward freeing a line, he was asked to stand back to allow the Coast Guard to do it. It wasn't a particularly pretty or smooth operation, but eventually we watched *Vigilance* turn toward the northeast with *Eva B.* tethered securely and closely behind.

I pulled the fenders aboard and stowed the small lines that had once held the *Eva B.* at our side as Cal put the engine in gear and headed toward Green Haven. Cal took one last look over his shoulder and pointed at the sky behind us with two fingers that squeezed a smoldering cigarette. "There," he said. "They've got an air search going. Nothing more we can do." The sight of the helicopter flying low over the water seemed to give Cal permission to leave the scene that trumped any from the Coast Guard. He pushed the throttle up to near full and concentrated on the landmass in the distance. Weird, I reflected, how thoughts of the missing man, Parker Alley, affected me. I was no stranger to missing, or even dead, people. But this was different. We had stumbled upon this without warning. Normally, I was the one to question witnesses. I was the one who would unravel the mystery. And leaving the scene with no answers weighed particularly heavy—like the leaded apron the dentist drapes over your torso before X-raying your teeth. Something said "foul play" to me. But I'd have to shake that thought, as there was no reason for any suspicion. A fisherman had been lost at sea. It happens. His body would wash up on the shore somewhere, and there would be closure. Perhaps the gnawing in my gut was hunger, I thought, as I pulled half a sandwich from my tote bag.

"Want half?" I asked Cal.

"Half of what? Half of half of a peanut butter sandwich I watched you eat the first half of three days ago?"

Cal teased, trying to lighten my mood. "Is that all you eat? You must have been raised in an orphanage or something. You're too young to have experienced the Depression. This food rationing thing must have come from your childhood, right?"

"No," I laughed. "I just don't like waste"—I hesitated—"of any kind."

"Well, you go ahead and enjoy it. Betty will have dinner ready by the time I get home." Cal's wife, Betty, is a great home cook. Cal chuckled a bit before adding, "I'll bet you walked to school barefoot, too. Never met such a penny-pincher in my life. Must be something planted deep in your head from childhood. You were taught the value of every dime, right?" My answer was a slow and silent savoring of the stale sandwich. Peanut butter and honey—the honey was a splurge I would not confess to Cal. Amused that he thought of my predilection for cutting financial corners as some sort of effect of trauma or a psychosis, I did nothing to deny either. I was tempted to explain to Cal how the thrift all my friends chided me for was indeed a result of my raising, but not in the way he assumed. My frugality was more of a rebellion to, rather than consequence of, the way I was raised. I relaxed and nibbled the edges of crust, putting on a display for Cal, who watched in disbelief as I nursed what anyone other than a prisoner of war would consume in two bites. The truth about my childhood financial situation was actually pretty funny, I thought, as the entrance to the channel leading to Green Haven Harbor came into view. I must have been all of seven or eight when my mother first taught me the value of money.

It began when I was in the second grade. I asked my mother if "we were rich." "Rich," it seemed at that age, was perhaps the greatest adjective that one could use to describe oneself. And I was absolutely delighted when she answered in the affirmative. Yes, we were rich. We were very rich. She could have left it at that, and I would have been happy. But my mother went on to define our particular kind of wealth. She explained that we were rich in health, happiness, and family love. And, she asked rhetorically, weren't we lucky to have all that? I didn't want to burst my mother's bubble, but I wanted to see bank statements. Money, it seemed, was of no consequence. We had happiness. I think it's fair to say that my personal obsession with financial security and extreme sense of thrift were shaped largely by my mother's "warped" perception of wealth. Still, I have been guided by it, I guess—as I haven't made the most lucrative career choices. For example, Mom's primer on wealth came back to haunt her when I began working for Archie for what she considered slave wages at the age of eleven. I could, she reminded me almost daily, make more money collecting cans and bottles. But, I argued, I was *happy* working on the dock and occasionally aboard the boat. And other than those few times Archie compensated me, I remained unemployed throughout high school—living on love, sustained by happiness, bolstered by kinship.

When my mother did have money, a check from the State of Florida, which she acted surprised to find in her mail on or around the first of every month for as far back as I could remember, she spent like the legendary drunken sailor. She'd tear open the envelope and fan the long yellow check in the air, yelling, "Pay dirt!" It always bothered me that she never saved a nickel for the rest of the month. It was a ritual. "Pay dirt! Come on, Janie! Let's get your brother cleaned up and go out on the town. What do you say?" We never returned home until we had spent the entire check. The remainder of the month we ate meals bought on food stamps, except for my school lunches, which Archie subsidized so that I could avoid the "free line." Oh, and fish. We ate a lot of fish that I brought home from work. Although my mother loved fresh seafood of any kind and referred to it as "brain food," she'd sometimes joke about wishing I'd find a job on a cattle ranch.

All of this reminiscence went down with the last swallow of sandwich, which I had chewed the mandatory thirty-two times. Suddenly the VHF radio came to life with, "Motor vessel *Asprella* calling the *Eva B.* Come in, Captain." The name of Parker Alley's boat brought me quickly back to the scene at hand. I looked at Cal for his reaction, but his eyes remained on the horizon. After a pause, the ship called again. "*Eva B., Eva B.*, the *Asprella* on channel sixteen. Channel one six, Captain. Come in, please."

Again, there was no visible sign that Cal was moved in any way by this new boat calling the *Eva B.*, but he must have sensed my anxiety as he finally said, "I thought the Coasties might respond. Guess not." Grabbing the microphone, Cal hesitated another few seconds to give the Coast Guard opportunity to answer the call. When they didn't, Cal keyed the mic and said, "*Asprella, Sea Pigeon*. Come in."

"*Asprella* back to the *Sea Pigeon*. Want to shift to channel seventy-three, Captain?"

"Roger." Cal pushed a button on the VHF, changing the channel to 73, and then hailed the *Asprella* again. When the ship's captain answered, Cal relayed that the *Eva B.* was "on the wrong end of a tow line." There was a short pause while this information was digested or discussed, and then the *Asprella*'s captain explained that the *Eva B.* had been hired as their pilot boat and was to meet them to pick up the ship's pilot after they were out of the shipping zone. I was unfamiliar with Maine state law, but knew that the federal government requires all ships to take on an additional captain licensed as a pilot to guide the ship through all hazards to navigation. The pilot would be delivered to the ship offshore of any area the ship must transit and outside of any headlands of navigational hazards. The pilot would be someone with "local knowledge" of the area. In this remote area of light shipping, I assumed there were no official pilot boats, so a lobster boat was used. The *Asprella* was now out of the danger zone, so the man piloting her needed a ride ashore. The pause was now on Cal's end of the conversation. "Are you in any hurry to get home?" he asked me. When I responded that I was not, Cal keyed the mic and offered his services to the *Asprella*. "But I'm going to Green Haven. The pilot will have to make arrangements to get home from there," Cal added.

"Roger, Captain. He'll be happier in Green Haven than he would be in Nova Scotia, which is our next stop. We're coming out of Mussel Ridge Channel now and will be heading due east."

"Roger. I'll intercept your course just south of Green Haven." And with this, Cal turned the *Sea Pigeon* back offshore. Within ten minutes we could see the *Asprella* heading toward us. As the ship grew near, I could see that she was a very large and well-maintained oil tanker. Seven hundred feet of hulking steel diminished Cal's boat to suit her name. I was at sea on the back of a pigeon. The bright yellow shell painted high on the ship's superstructure was further evidence that she was indeed a member of the oil fleet. The ship's captain called Cal with some instructions, basically telling him that his intentions were to maintain course and speed at eighty-five degrees and twelve knots, allowing Cal to come along on the *Asprella*'s port side. On that side, just ahead of the bridge, there would be a rope ladder directly under which Cal was instructed to press the side of *Sea Pigeon* against some heavy chaffing gear and fenders. A deckhand would be the first to descend the ladder, lending assistance to the pilot if needed, the captain explained. Once the pilot was safely aboard, the deckhand would return to the *Asprella,* and Cal should pull away. To these instructions Cal replied, "Roger." Knowing that we had just been through a similar drill capturing the circling *Eva B.*, I had great confidence in Cal's boat-handling skills even when running up against the huge tanker. But I was relieved to not be the one jumping ship this time.

It went just as the captain suggested it should. Cal maneuvered alongside and against the rugged fenders just under the rope ladder, which was more of a net of coarse webbing, and held position there using the throttle to keep us against the *Asprella*'s hull. A small, sharp-faced man scrambled down and straddled the gap between the two boats, keeping one hand and one foot on the webbing. A canvas tote bag was lowered on a hook to the man who took it with his free hand. Next, the pilot appeared high above us. He was a much bigger man and was more careful on his way down. He looked before each step to the next rung and seemed reluctant to force the release of each handhold. Finally, he stepped onto the rail with a hand grasping the deckhand's forearm, grabbed the tote bag, and jumped into the middle of the deck with a flat-footed thud. As soon as the deckhand saw the pilot safely on deck, he waved and scurried back up the ladder, as agile as could be. "Adios," the pilot yelled cheerily after the deckhand, who quickly scaled the tanker's mountainous wall. Then under his breath he muttered, "Fuckin' monkey."

We were quiet as Cal pulled away from the expansive steel tanker, I suppose because it was a bit tense. The speed of the massive ship as it increased throttle was quite amazing, I thought. Something that big shouldn't move that fast. When we passed her stern, I noticed the *Asprella*'s hailing port was Honduras. High in the rigging

I saw the Honduran flag and recalled what I had learned in grade school regarding the significance of its markings. Blue stripes represented the Pacific Ocean and Caribbean Sea and white was the land between them. I couldn't remember what the five stars depicted. I closed my eyes and saw flags from Cuba, Nicaragua, Haiti, and Honduras surrounding Old Glory on the classroom walls of Henry Flagler Elementary. Flagler, of railroad fame, was the first lesson every year—a way to create school pride and unite the factions of kids from the host of countries whose flags adorned our walls. A refugee of sorts, I fit right in with my Latino classmates, who hailed from every ethnic corner of the neighborhood. Ours was an incidental and circumstantial cultural integration— while desegregation busing was being enforced elsewhere, we were a thriving melting pot of inner-city kids unaware of *Brown v. Board of Education.* Funny, all I remembered about Henry Flagler now was that he married three times and died after falling down the stairs.

Once we were in the clear of the *Asprella*'s wake and pointed back in the direction of Green Haven, the pilot introduced himself with quite a flourish of smiles and enthusiasm, not to mention volume. "Hello, folks! The name's Kelley, Willard Kelley. I can't thank youuuuu enough. What a lovely daaaaay, isn't it?" The only urge stronger than the one to plug my ears was the one to hold my nose. Wow, I thought, Willard Kelley has been nipping something. He wasn't, as far I could tell, intoxicated. But there were signs other than his breath that indicated that he had been drinking heavily in the not too distant past. He appeared to have sobered up with a shower as his hair was slicked back and he was heavily perfumed with aftershave: Old Spice, I thought. We exchanged names and handshakes, after which Kelley referred to Cal and me using our full names, Jane Bunker and Cal Dunham, and persistently drew out a random single-syllable word to the point of irritation.

Kelley was a mammoth of a man. He towered over me and moved in close to talk. "So, my friend Parker had to be towed by the Coast Guaaaaard, did you say? My, my, that must certainly have ruined his daaaaay. Probably didn't sell his lobsters yet, either. Too bad. Bad newwwwws."

"You're a friend of Parker Alley?" I asked.

"Well, not a close friend. But he's been my pilot boat for years. Nice maaaaan. Do you know him?"

"No," I said, still wanting to know more about the missing fisherman. After a thoughtful pause to wait for Cal to launch into the story of how we happened upon the *Eva B.*, I realized that Cal was not in the mood for conversation. He had turned on the radar, as it was getting dark, and was focused on navigating us into Green Haven. I thought it might be inconsiderate to allow Kelley to believe that Parker Alley's bad luck was as simple as a broken-down boat. Thinking I could get information by giving information, I told the story, beginning with our trip and reason for going to Cobble Harbor that morning. Kelley listened with interest and interjected a few questions for more detail. He winced at appropriate places and shook his head in disbelief when I got to the part where we found the circling boat with nobody aboard. Kelley seemed genuinely saddened by the loss of a man with whom he had worked for so long.

My ploy to learn more about Parker Alley was a complete failure. The apparent loss of his business associate seemed to have shaken Kelley into a silent mode. As Cal made the boat fast to the dock in the inner harbor, where I had met him so many hours ago, Kelley crossed himself, mumbled what I interpreted as a prayer, and wiped a tear from the corner of his eye. Before heaving himself onto the rail and then onto the wharf, Kelley took a deep breath and exhaled loudly. "Thank you both for everything. I very much appreciate your caaaaaaare and time in helping meeeee and for what you did for Parker Alley." He reached into his canvas tote and pulled out a bottle of Johnnie Walker Black Label, offering it to Cal.

"No thanks. I don't drink." If only Cal knew that this was the favorite scotch of Winston Churchill, I thought, perhaps he'd accept the gift of thanks. Although I prefer the Green Label, I hoped the bottle would be offered to me. It was not. If I was going to splurge on anything, it would definitely be truly great whiskey. Johnnie disappeared into the depths of the bag, where he clinked against whatever other distilled treats were cloistered within.

"You're a better maaaaan than I, Cal Dunham. Thanks again. Now I'm off to fiiiiiind a lady friend. A gal in every port, right, ol' boy? I'm in no rush to find my way back to Cobble Harbor. All work and noooo play . . ." With this he snickered and banged Cal on the back. "Just my luck, I'm walking distance to the chicken coop. Any port in a storm. No offense, Jane Bunker."

We said our goodbyes and watched Willard Kelley disappear on foot up the dock and into the parking lot. "What a rig," Cal said with a smile as he snapped taut the hitch he'd made around a piling with the stern line. "I probably should have taken that jug and given it to you. Sorry I didn't."

"I like single malts. Don't usually drink blended whiskey," I said with an air of superiority that I am sure went unappreciated. I climbed over the rail and onto the dock.

"I wouldn't know the difference," Cal said as he joined me on the dock. We walked to Cal's truck, where he opened the door and asked, "What's next?"

Although my heart wanted to search for Parker Alley, I knew that Cal was asking about the job we'd begun in Cobble Harbor this morning. "I'll file the paperwork for the insurance claim and the police report and let you know if there will be follow-up with another trip. Other than that, I'll wait for the next assignment and call you when I need a ride. Thanks for everything, Cal. We'll settle up when I get a check from the Sheriff's Department."

"Okay. Ride home?"

Knowing that a walk up the hill would stretch my legs and clear my mind, I declined the offer of a ride and bid Cal good night. I slung the handles of my bag onto my shoulder, tucked my hands into my hip pockets, and struck out for home. Soon it would be my first winter in

Maine—or at least the first one since I had been old enough to pay attention. I anticipated the cooler weather with a childish excitement. God, I thought, what if I couldn't tolerate the cold? All of those snowbirds couldn't be wrong. Snow angels and hot chocolate could be overrated. Autumn was certainly splendid, I thought, as the tempo of music through an open window quickened my pace. I hustled by the darkened doorways of the coffee shop and past the Old Maids. I imagined Marlena and Marilyn strategizing how to best hook customers into unnecessary purchases as they doted on their litter of Scottish Folds, their prized and odd cats that were fixtures as permanent as the cash register in the gals' all-purpose store.

The local businesses had shortened their hours, and would further reduce the times they were open by Thanksgiving, as the seasonal residents had left Green Haven in droves on Labor Day and were still trickling away. Many of those who would stay took great pride in their status as year-rounders, but the cachet of this had evaded me so far. I hoped it was not testimony to their toughness or need for survival skills. Full-time residents of Green Haven were quick to let you know how many generations their family had endured here. With this in mind, I realized that winter might be very difficult to bear. I'd soon know if the hardiness boasted of by the natives of this town was genetic or conditioned.

I decided not to attempt to evade the motion-sensing lights in my landlords' gift shop and sneak to my apartment unnoticed, so I walked right through the Vickersons' front door after a knock and yelled, "Hello. Anybody home?"

"Jane! Of course we're home. Where else would we be at happy hour? Come in, come in," Mrs. V called back in a tone that hinted that happy hour was well under way. I entered, closing the door behind me, and found the elderly couple whom I had come to adore—in spite of their many quirks and annoying habits—sipping highballs and splitting attention between the local nightly news and the stereo. "Where have you been, girl?" asked Alice. And before I could answer she added, "Henry, get Jane a drink."

"Great. Thanks, Mr. V. It's been a long day," I said and sank into the recliner that they always seemed to leave vacant for me.

"What'll you have?" Henry asked as he headed for the liquor cabinet.

"Whatever you're drinking will be fine, thanks."

Henry hesitated in mid-stride and reached for the volume knob on the stereo. "I love this part!" Turning the set back up, he sang along, "I picked a good one. It looked like it could run." Although he was off-key, Henry was right on tempo with Marty Robbins's lamenting of his lost love Feleena. Henry pumped a fist in the air and announced, "That man is a musical genius!"

"Turn that down, dear," Alice whined. "Jane and I want to visit and it's almost time for the weather . . . Kevin Mannix . . . Channel six. *He's* the genius." Henry did as Alice requested and made his way to the well-stocked liquor cabinet. He returned seconds later with a healthy pour of some brown beverage over ice, handed it to me with a cocktail napkin printed with a phone number for the Betty Ford Center, and relaxed on his end of the couch. "Now, if you haven't had dinner, Jane, we have a mussel soufflé in the oven that'll be done in twenty minutes."

I considered the combination of mussels and eggs. I considered the options that might come from my fridge. "Sounds great, Mrs. V. Is this another experiment for your *All Mussel Cookbook*?" While Alice explained the recipe—ingredients and inspiration—I swirled my drink with hopes of diluting it. The *All Mussel Cookbook* had been in the works for years and the Vickersons, despite having cooked mussel dishes every night since the book's inception, seemed no closer to finishing it than when they started.

"And Henry found the most gorgeous, petite mussels right below Horseman's Point. We thought the small ones would work better in a soufflé." Alice had certainly been blessed with the gift of gab, I thought. It was incredible how she was simply never at a loss for something to say. "Of course, I couldn't go with him. Art came to visit today, and stayed." I knew that this was code for Alice having had a bad time with her arthritis, and interjected with a sympathetic groan and frown. "You'll be glad to know that I took your advice and began my medical journal yesterday," she continued as she placed her hand on a notebook on the end table beside her. "I haven't kept a diary in years, but I think you're right. It will be helpful to my doctors to see what I have been experiencing between visits." She handed the notebook to me as she continued with her schedule of upcoming appointments. The cover of the notebook showed a Raggedy Ann doll to which Alice had added a hand-drawn thermometer, Band-Aids, crutches, and facial stitches.

I half listened to Alice and thought I heard Henry snoring on the far end of the couch they shared. That was the best thing about Alice's monologues, I thought. She didn't expect any participation whatsoever. In fact, if I had something to say, which was rare, I knew to rudely interrupt. That was absolutely acceptable. I kept an eye on the television and was captivated when the ticker that ran along the bottom of the screen promised an upcoming story about a missing fisherman. At least Parker Alley is getting a bit of airtime, I thought, as Alice defined fibromyalgia. Somewhere between Alice's unexplained pain and chronic fatigue, the newscaster gained my full attention. "In a bizarre twist of cruel fate, a Cobble Harbor fisherman went missing from his boat today. Authorities have not yet found the body of thirty-nine-year-old Parker Alley. The Coast Guard has suspended their search until morning. Alley was the father of Jason Alley, the recently deceased teen whose death is a suspected overdose and whose funeral is tomorrow. Our thoughts and prayers go out to the entire Alley family and Cobble Harbor community."

4

I FORCED MYSELF OUT OF BED, teetering between feeling good about the extra hour of sleep I'd logged and a little slovenly about not having been up before the sun. Maybe it was the after-dinner drink I had accepted, as a deterrent to retiring too early, that slowed my usual morning routine. I pulled open the window shades. The grayness outside did nothing to lighten the funk in which I found myself. Precipitation so light it appeared to hover rather than spritz the ground distorted the view of the harbor in a way that seemed fitting. Yes, I thought, this is a great day for sadness and grieving and tears. A stone's throw to the east, the cozy little community of Cobble Harbor was fully exposed to all elements and emotions today. Missing persons and overdosed teens were commonplace where I come from. But even in the short while I had lived in Green Haven I had begun not only to understand, but to feel the shame and disgrace families and whole communities experience when illegal activity is close at hand. I felt bad. Well, maybe more like sad. Weird, I thought, how a mere one-hour difference in the usual start of the day could throw me out of sync. Or there was the possibility that I was changing.

My past in Miami was littered with similar incidents and statistics. The kid next door could have been killed by a rival gang, an overdose, or just a random drive-by shooting. I wouldn't learn his name. I'd know only how many others had gone the same way in whichever week he had gone down. I wouldn't even know his case number. My concentration then was at the other end of the chain—the top of the chain. I knew the life histories of all the major drug barons, all the traffickers in illegal immigrants, prostitutes, and weapons. I dealt with kingpins. I studied them. I knew what their middle initials stood for. I didn't care to know how old the deceased neighbor was, or what his hobbies were, or what he looked like stretched out in the coffin. How did the death of Jason Alley, which I learned of only last night, and the disappearance and probable death of his father pull the shades on my world into which thousands of others had never cast a shadow? Was this the compassion I had always been accused of not having? After twenty-odd years in Miami criminal justice, had my move here finally softened the stone-hearted "Let's get the bad guys at any cost" gal my colleagues loathed? Did I really lie awake last night worrying about the mother and wife of Jason and Parker? Lillian, was it? God, did I actually remember her name? I *had* changed.

Even though I had overslept, it was still too early to check in with either of my bosses. Mr. Dubois, my immediate superior at Eastern Marine Safety Consultants, was never available to answer the phone until ten. And the Knox County Sheriff's Department wouldn't have anyone manning the desk for incoming calls for another two hours. And, no, it was not okay to dial the emergency number just because you are an impatient, early riser. I had learned that the hard way, twice. With a little time to kill, a mood to lighten, and a need for caffeine, I knew the Harbor Café was the one-stop shop to satisfy all.

Three steps out the door and into the parking lot, I realized the weather was worse than I first gathered from the upstairs window. It was raw; not just wet, but cold. I pulled the front of my unbuttoned cardigan together to close the gap and hustled to my car. Sliding behind the wheel, I rummaged through my tote bag for the ignition key. I had not yet become accustomed to leaving doors unlocked. I shivered and dug deeper into the bag, frustrated by all of the accumulated clutter I had picked up since the last shaking out. I had never been one to lose things, so was quick to hit the panic button when whatever I needed didn't surface immediately. It was no use. I had emptied the bag onto the seat beside me and there was no key. "Damn," I whispered. I'd have to walk. As I pushed the door open, I noticed the key sitting in the ignition. Wow, I really had changed, I thought. I had better keep this departure from the norm to myself, I thought with a hint of glee as I turned the key and stomped on the accelerator.

I'd had numerous conversations with fellow Green Haveners about this practice of leaving keys in cars, and was consistently on the losing end of what nearly always turned into a debate about safety and risk of theft. They scowled when I admonished them for their negligence.

They laughed at the prospect of anyone stealing my Duster. Apparently, no one would ever be quite that desperate. They were amused with my observation that three quarters of Green Haveners drove vehicles listed in the Top Ten Most Stolen. They ignored my tips, including keeping packages out of sight, leaving windows up, putting house keys on a separate key ring, and parking in well-lit, busy areas. They barely tolerated the Post-its I stuck to their steering wheels with notes questioning their obliviousness to matters of security. Now it appeared that I had joined the ranks of the negligent. I had never been described as laid back. I was curious how far my metamorphosis from uptight cop to anarchic Mainer would go.

Absent the summer congestion, Main Street was downright roomy, I thought, as I prepared to swing wide into the parking area in front of the café. Clyde Leeman, who had grown dear to me in spite of being a major nuisance in a village idiot sort of way, stood on the sidewalk and motioned me into a spot directly opposite the coffee shop's entrance. "Cut 'er to the right. Hard right. Keep comin'," Clydie yelled so that I could hear him through the tight windows. His right hand swiveled at the wrist and rotated rapidly toward his face. "Little more. Little more. That's it. Easy." I was on the verge of laughter. There were no cars in the spots on either side of where I was parking. When he signaled me to stop by drawing an index finger across his throat, I jumped on the brake pedal so hard the Duster rocked back and forth on worn-out shocks before finally coming to rest with the front bumper against Clydie's knees. His belt buckle, a snarling bulldog bearing teeth that spelled MAC, might make a nice hood ornament, I thought.

"Hey, thanks, Clyde," I said as I shut and locked the Duster's door behind me. "Are you on your way in or out?" Clyde stood forged to open the entrance to the café.

"I'm out. She gave me the boot before I even finished my second cup." Clyde seemed to take pride in being ejected from the café by Audrey, the young woman who managed and ruled the small business with an iron fist. "I ought to complain to the owners. But I wouldn't want her to get fired. She's in one particular foul mood this morning, Miss Bunker. Be careful."

"Thanks for the warning." I nodded goodbye to Clyde as he closed the door between us a little harder than was required. The cowbells that dangled at mid-door clanged loudly, compelling the attention of the café's only two customers. The Old Maids, Marilyn and Marlena, were bellied up to their usual places at the breakfast counter.

"Who is it?" yelled Audrey angrily from the kitchen.

"It's Jane," answered the ladies in unison.

"Oh, good!" came the reaction from behind the louvered doors that hid the kitchen from view. Audrey sounded genuinely pleased that I had arrived. I like Audrey, too. A feisty, hardworking girl of about nineteen, Audrey had formed an unlikely friendship with me. The fact that she looked like a punk rocker no longer fazed me. The fact that she didn't care what I thought about anything did. Sure, she has tattoos, pierced body parts, and spiked hair, but I still saw a bit of my youth in Audrey. She's stubborn. Just like me. She is the reason I've made the café part of my morning routine—that and the fact that I am not a cook but also understand that breakfast is the one meal not to be missed.

I joined Marilyn and Marlena at the counter and exchanged the usual pleasantries, then bemoaned the gloomy weather. Audrey came crashing through the swinging doors with a smile that stole the scene from what appeared to be her newly dyed, jet-black hair. "Hey, Jane," she said as she grabbed the glass coffeepot from its warming pad, flipped the mug right-side up on the paper placemat at my section of the counter, and filled it to the brim. "What can I get you, the special?"

Oh, I had become so predictable, I thought. Cal's comments about pinching pennies had struck a nerve. Everyone must think of me as the biggest cheapskate in town. "No, I would like eggs Benedict, please. Poached sort of medium."

"But you always have the special." Her voice went up at the end, as if she were asking a question, like Audrey was wondering if I was all right.

Delighted with her concern, I smiled and said, "I know. I just feel like eggs Benedict this morning."

"You're kidding, right? Eggs Benedict? They're eight fifty. With the tip, that'll cost you a ten spot."

Oh, I hadn't realized breakfast could cost so much. Maybe I would reconsider. No, I wouldn't let Audrey sway me. "I know it's a little splurge. I like eggs Benedict

and I haven't had them in a while. Please?" Why I was
defending my breakfast order, I had no idea.

Audrey placed her hands on her hips and glared at
me, unwilling to give up. "You order the special every
day, without even asking what it is. Now suddenly you
are in the mood for the most expensive thing on the
menu? What's wrong? Marlena and Marilyn both had
the special for two ninety-nine apiece." Audrey turned
her attention to the Old Maids with some expectation of
backup.

"We did. Both of us," confirmed Marilyn.

"It was good, too," added Marlena.

"This is weird," I said and then chuckled. "Okay. You
win. I've changed my mind. I'd like the special, please." I
raised my coffee mug in a salute to the three women and
chuckled again as Audrey disappeared into the kitchen.
"What was that about?" I asked.

Marilyn leaned close and spoke softly. "The cook
called in sick."

"Again," added Marlena.

"Audrey's filling in at the stove until he recovers,"
Marilyn confided in a whisper and jerked a thumb toward the kitchen.

"With any luck, that'll be before the lunch crowd
comes in." Both women clasped their hands together and
glanced at the ceiling as if God lived in the attic. I didn't
know whether their prayers went to the attention of the
cook, Audrey, or the customers looking for lunch.

"Oh. Why didn't she just say so?" I asked. When I got
no answer other than a stare and a shrug that I took as a

reasonable explanation from adults for any actions of a nineteen-year-old girl, I asked, "So, what's the special?"

Now it was the ladies' turn to laugh. They shared a look between them before Marlena said, "Toast."

"Toast! Three-dollar toast?"

"White, whole wheat, or rye?" The question came from behind the doors.

Assuming that Audrey couldn't see me, I raised my hands in surrender. "Rye?" I asked permission.

"That figures." Disgust oozed through the slats of the door.

The next five minutes were filled with banging and slamming of untold things, resulting in a range of sounds including obscenities. The three of us anxiously awaited Audrey's return from what she must certainly have considered hell. Marlena made what amounted to a false start toward the door as Marilyn yanked the hem of her jacket, pulling her back onto the red vinyl upholstered stool between us. Majorly relieved that I would not be left without witnesses to Audrey's wrath, I stood, reached for the pot, and poured three fresh cups of coffee.

"It's probably just her age," Marilyn said as she dumped sugar into her cup and stirred. "Of course, we've been saying that since she learned to talk." Our laughter melted the frost from our side of the swinging doors and we were quickly engaged in warm, meaningless conversation.

When Audrey burst through the doors carrying a tray over one shoulder, the hush was immediate. Smiles vanished without a trace. "Okay." Audrey glanced at the contents of the tray. "Let's see ... who ordered the toast?" She looked at me and continued, "Oh yes. You wanted the special, didn't you?" I didn't dare open my mouth. I nodded. Setting a plate with four slices of rye toast down in front of me, she said, "You do realize that you're seated in the tweed-only section." The Old Maids were, as always, wearing tweed blazers. Again, I didn't dare open my mouth.

"Was that a comment about our clothes?" Marlena sounded a bit insulted.

"No, that was a comment about Jane's. She's the one not up to code." Audrey reached back onto the tray and set down a plate of cheeses and luncheon meats, then a plate with butter and individual jellies. Next came a bowl of mixed fruit and finally a bowl of cottage cheese. And even some fried eggs.

"Wow, thanks for recommending the special. This looks great," I said before Marlena or Marilyn could react to Audrey's comment about their clothes. "All this for two ninety-nine? Nice." I meant it, too. Audrey had pulled out all the stops.

"That's a lot more special than our specials were," complained Marlena.

Audrey's hands went onto her hips again, a sure sign that she was preparing to fire another shot. I focused on buttering the rye toast and hoped that Audrey would back down. I held my breath until Audrey said nonchalantly, "So, get over it." Thankfully they did get over it. That was the end of the snapping for the time being as the ladies discussed safer things, such as the slowing of

Main Street business since Labor Day. That was something the people who worked either side of Green Haven's main thoroughfare could agree upon. I couldn't
help but think that Audrey wasn't herself this morning.
She had always been a caustic, sharp-tongued smart-ass.
And, of course, she could cook, but would have been
mad about having to man the café solo. But it wasn't like
her to be mean to the harmless Old Maids. I knew better
than to challenge her or ask why she might be out of
sorts. I blamed my own sour attitude on the weather, but
doubted that the tough, resilient Audrey was sensitive to
a little cold and rain. Although she was busy chopping
and prepping everything that needed to be done before
lunch, she still held up her end of the conversation in the
way I was accustomed to and enjoyed. It wasn't until the
conversation slowed to the usual drivel about our individual daily agendas that Audrey confessed the reason
for her mood. "I was supposed to go to a funeral today.
Now I'm stuck doing the cook's job so I can't make it."

"Who died?" Marilyn asked.

"A friend."

"Oh, I'm sorry, honey. Was it an accident?" asked
Marilyn.

"Yes, I think so. I heard he overdosed on heroin."

"Jason Alley," I said without any inflection of inquiry.
Audrey confirmed and wanted to know how I knew his
name. "News last night," I said. "How close were you to
him? I mean, how well did you know him?" I tried to
sound truly concerned and I was; I didn't want Audrey
to think that I was simply gathering information for an

investigation. This wasn't my case; I really hoped Audrey could tell I was genuinely sympathetic.

Audrey explained that she hadn't seen Jason in over a year and that they had been members of the same youth group back when they were younger. As he lived all the way over in Cobble Harbor, they didn't ever run into each other, she said.

"Heroin in Cobble Harbor!" Marilyn exclaimed. "Unbelievable."

"You'd better believe it," Audrey remarked. "It's everywhere. It's here."

"In Green Haven? Really? Heroin?" Marilyn looked stunned.

"Heroin. Heaven dust. Aunt Hazel." Audrey recited some of the nicer common slang.

"Hell dust, poison, slime." I was able to remember more fitting terms for heroin.

Audrey countered with "Hard candy, hero, sugar."

Not to be outdone, I recalled, "Smack, shit, dirt, dope, junk."

"Sweet Jesus, Joy flakes, dyno, white china," Audrey challenged.

"Judas" was all I could come up with.

"Judas? I've never heard that one."

"Oh sure, Judas. Heroin . . . the friend that betrays you. Was Jason chasing the tiger, or was he a channel swimmer?" I asked in reference to how he took it—smoking or injecting.

"Whoa." Audrey put her hands in the air, palms facing me. "I know when I'm in over my head. I'm there. I have no idea what you're talking about. I read a lot. I don't use drugs. I didn't know Jason did. We were friends a long time ago. I'm not going to his funeral. Okay?" For a minute, I had slipped back into the hard, cold Jane mode. I took a deep breath and remembered the victim, coaxing myself back to my newly found sensitive side. The Old Maids were still stuck in the horrible thought that there were illegal drugs in their hometown. When they questioned this again, Audrey explained that not only was heroin available, but that it was very affordable. "It's as cheap as beer. Or so I've heard." This did nothing but add to the ladies' dismay.

Audrey was holding her own, but I thought I could contribute something more to the conversation from my experience in Miami. "A big part of the problem is politics and the war on drugs. Law enforcement's concentration on cocaine and marijuana has allowed heroin to slip through the cracks," I explained. "Heroin was once known as the poor black man's drug. There wasn't a lot of pressure to stop it. Let 'em die. That was the attitude. Now middle-class kids are using it in increasing numbers."

"Politics, law enforcement . . ." When her hands slid to her waist I knew Audrey was ramping up for confrontation, I could just tell. "They ought to just legalize all drugs and be done with it."

Oh, she had trod on sacred ground. "Legalize heroin? Are you out of your mind? It is so addictive! The body builds a tolerance, calling for more and more to achieve the high. That's how people die," I said.

"Physical dependence is a problem," Audrey agreed. "But the same can be said of alcohol, tobacco, sleep aids. People die using those to excess, too. Poppy seeds have been around since time began. There's never been a culture that's denied people the right to get lit up."

I couldn't believe what I was hearing. "But heroin is illegal. No one has the *right* to use it. Someone needs to go to jail," I said, sounding more like my old self.

"Of course, that's law enforcement's answer to everything. Put 'em in jail," Audrey said. "One cell costs fifty thousand dollars to build and more than twenty thousand a year to fill and maintain. Our prisons are overcrowded now with drug offenders. And my friend is still dead."

I then noticed that Audrey was crying. She wasn't mad at me. I don't think she even believed what she was saying. She's just one of those people—like me—who argue when they're sad. "Someone will go to jail. You have my word on that." Maybe I hadn't changed.

5

ALTHOUGH I WOULD NEVER AGREE that the solution to illegal drugs was to legalize them, Audrey and I had found a small piece of common ground regarding drugs and law enforcement. Sure, the small-time dealer who would push heroin cut with flea powder to experimenting, tormented teens in order to support his own habit needed to be put out of business. But that, in my opinion, was treating the symptom, not the problem. Heroin junkies are like weeds. Once they take hold in an area, eradication is nearly impossible. Arresting his supplier would not bring justice to Jason Alley. It might delay, but would not stop, the next overdose. We needed to get his supplier's supplier.

My tendency (detractors would call it a handicap) to focus solely on the larger picture was something I had long ago convinced myself was an asset. I would not get bogged down in the small details of Cobble Harbor's drug scene. Law enforcement officers always vow to get to the bottom of the problem. My intention was always to get to the *top* of a problem. As I slid behind the wheel of the Duster, I wondered to what degree Audrey had played me. We had certainly volleyed plenty of issues over the net in the last three months; the focus from either end was always an attempt to gain information about the other's past without relinquishing much of our own. Audrey had always done homework, knowing more of my life in Miami than I did of hers in Green Haven. Of course, a nineteen-year-old doesn't have as much past as a forty-one-year-old professional who has spent more than twenty years in the public eye. But from what I had gathered, Audrey had crammed a lot of experience into her nearly two decades of life. She was remarkably mature and easy to talk to and confide in—rather rare in my limited female friendships. She knew the career I had left in Miami. She knew some of the whys. She knew how to push everyone's buttons to line them up and march to her drummer. Although I was well aware of Audrey's wily ways, I couldn't seem to resist falling prey to them this time. Sure, I could ignore the weeds in my backyard. But finding and turning off the breeze they had blown in on was my forte. I guessed Audrey knew this—and knew just how to talk me into taking action.

The first order of business, I thought, was to check in with the Sheriff's Department and see who had been assigned to investigate Jason Alley's death. With any luck, I would be asked to assist. If that ploy should prove unsuccessful, I could get to Cobble Harbor under the guise of the missing person case. Perhaps I could work with Marine Patrol in the search for Parker Alley. Surely my supervisor at the Knox County Sheriff's Department would be inclined to assign the "new gal" this mundane chore, which would seem to consist primarily in generating a mound of paperwork. And, if all else failed, I could

drive to Cobble Harbor in the role of "insurance lady."
Wouldn't it be responsible and professional to follow up
on the vandalism aboard *Quest*? And couldn't I then
broaden the scope of my investigation as I saw fit? I entered my apartment and headed straight for the phone,
excited about the prospect of getting back to what I considered the "real work" that I had sworn off in my haste to
get out of Dodge. So much for leaving the past behind.

   The phone's answering machine flashed a red number "2" on its display, indicating, to my surprise, that I
had received two calls in the last ninety minutes. I hadn't
received two calls in the past ninety *days,* I thought. Of
course, the main reason for the shortage of incoming calls
was the lack of outgoing calls. I was way overdue with a
call to my baby brother, Wally. That call would have
to wait, I thought, until I had more time. The first
message was from the very impatient Mr. Dubois, who
always started recordings with a big, disgusted sigh
and a comment about my never being home. Tempted
to skip ahead to the next message, I hesitated long
enough to be ordered to Cobble Harbor on behalf of
the missing Parker Alley's marine insurance company.
"Recent activity in the form of policy changes in Mr.
Alley's life insurance is causing some anxiety with the
underwriters . . . suspicion, really. Of course, we've
been hired to find some evidence that Alley killed himself as there is a suicide exclusion in term policies. Maybe
he left a note or said something to someone. His kid OD'd
last Wednesday. So, there's motive. When the body is
recovered there may be something to rule out accidental

death. Make it a priority." A click followed by the beep and a computerized voice stating the date and time gave me just seconds to appreciate the fact that I wouldn't need to make up an excuse to visit Cobble Harbor again.

The second message was from the Knox County Sheriff's Department and was another assignment requiring me to go to Cobble Harbor as soon as possible. There had been a report of a planned protest in the form of fishing boats blockading the only entrance to and exit from the harbor. The Sheriff's Department was responsible for keeping the protest peaceful, and as this was my territory I was expected to go. "A presence is all that's needed. We don't expect any problems." The tone suggested that the person leaving the message anticipated resistance on my part; like going all the way to Cobble Harbor was an enormous inconvenience. I wondered whether the fishermen were blockading in protest of new regulation or aquaculture. It didn't matter. I had just been given a second excuse to poke around and ask questions. So it was definitely no skin off my back.

I picked up the receiver to call Cal, then remembered the weather. We'd be bucking against easterly wind all the way if we took the *Sea Pigeon*. It might just be faster to drive. I hung the receiver back in its cradle. But I would need to buy gas in Ellsworth and gas is expensive. The phone was again against my ear. Of course, I would be reimbursed for travel expenses. I hesitated, the phone resting on my shoulder. A boat might come in handy to break up the blockade. But it would be an awfully damp, rough ride. Cal might appreciate another day's pay. If I went alone, I wouldn't have concerns about Cal's getting home in time for dinner. One if by land, two if by sea . . . I dialed Cal's number. No answer and no machine on the other end put my indecision into remission. I gathered a few things, including my badge, department-issued hand-gun (Glock model 22.40 S&W semiautomatic), and rain gear, threw them into my tote bag, and bolted back down the stairs and into the Duster.

I hadn't had much windshield time lately, I thought as I drove through town. Everything in Green Haven was so accessible on foot that I rarely used my old, faithful car. That would change with the weather. I flipped on the windshield wipers. The mooing sound from under the hood was a reminder that the wiper motor was on its last leg, and the smear directly at eye level indicated a need for new blades. This could be a long ride, I thought. Yesterday, when I had looked at a road map, I estimated the drive between Green Haven and Cobble Harbor to be two hours, while a boat ride was a mere seventeen miles. By land, the trip was the equivalent of driving the outer limits of a giant horseshoe rather than cutting across from tip to tip. When the mooing cow morphed to a rooster crowing at dawn I turned on the fan to help de-fog the windows and to drown out the barnyard noises made by the decrepit wiper motor; this resulted in a face full of dust and tiny particles that I imagined must have been bits of dead flying insects.

Before long I was driving the causeway leaving Green Haven proper and so entranced in fleshing out the shreds of information left on my answering machine that I was no longer annoyed by the noise or poor visibility. Pondering the notion of a boat blockade, I recalled hearing about many such protests in recent years; mainly fishing boats making last-ditch attempts to derail government regulations. It was never a victory dance, but more of a surrender ritual, and I doubted that the Cobble Harbor blockade would be an exception. It wouldn't amount to much, I was certain. This wasn't at all like Greenpeace versus France in 1985. The *Rainbow Warrior* was blown up and sunk by the French government as a permanent solution to the environmentalists' use of it to blockade shipping channels as a protest against nuclear testing. You would have thought that would have discouraged Greenpeace. But they built *Rainbow Warrior II* and she has been showing up in environmental pressure cookers ever since she first splashed water at her launching. Then I remembered a news story about surfers in Hawaii forming a human chain to stop the entrance into their harbor of a Superferry. Their gripe was that the speed of the ferry would endanger whales. So they put themselves in its path in protest. That didn't do much for the public's opinion of the surfers' sanity. Given the water temperature in Maine, I figured the Cobble Harbor fishermen would remain aboard their boats.

Deep in thought, I glanced at the fuel gauge and then at my surroundings. I was already in the middle of Ellsworth. Ellsworth, being the only gas-selling town along the way, was quite busy this morning. I decided to wait until the return trip to fill my tank, since the rain was coming down harder now. Peaceful protest wasn't a bad thing, I supposed. And trying to stop it might be seen as censorship on the high seas. Even a motley group of fishermen has the right to protest. I recalled recently hearing Green Haven lobstermen complaining of pending gear restrictions and modifications meant to protect whales. Whales, it seemed to me, find themselves at the heart of a lot of discord—counter to their nature. To protest any regulation that even remotely helps whales is foolhardy, I thought. The only good that comes from such activity is a bit of solidarity among the sure-to-fail protestors. And it seemed to me that Cobble Harbor could use a little kumbaya in the midst of the sadness that I was sure shrouded them after the loss of a son and father so tragically and unexpectedly.

Until the body of Parker Alley was recovered and put to rest, though, there might be some degree of unrest in Cobble Harbor. In a small town, closure is needed for everyone, not just the next of kin. Following today's funeral for his son, the community of Cobble Harbor would be embroiled in the search for Parker. But I wouldn't be surprised, I thought, as the road parted acres of spruce grown so thick individual trees were indistinguishable, if Parker Alley's body had been found by the time I arrived.

I eased up on the gas pedal as the road transformed from a route with an official number to "secondary." No doubt the Coast Guard helicopters were back on the scene with their infrared ability. Infrared cameras could detect temperature differences of less than one degree. Of course, the gradient between a body and the ocean would become imperceptible once the body assumed the temperature of the water in which it was submerged. The best chance of success with that method had passed, I knew. And temperature would truly be irrelevant once the body sank. Still, after a body goes under, decomposition creates gases that will refloat the corpse, except when the water is extremely cold. In spite of all the evidence obtained through years of collecting, the activity of corpses in water is not an exact science. Although people always comb beaches looking for what the tide may have left, in this case I doubted Parker Alley's body would travel that far. Drowning victims were usually found very close to where they drowned. You don't work coastal crime scenes for as long as I had and not know these things. People disappear; corpses do not. Parker's body would show up. And the Coast Guard would probably find it.

A sign indicated twelve more miles to Cobble Harbor. I could become public enemy number one, I realized, if word got out that I was being compensated to investigate Parker Alley's death with the hope of foiling payout of his life insurance benefits to the grieving widow. Although that would never be my prime motive, convincing emotionally stressed strangers that my purposes were noble would be tricky. I would be wise to wear my deputy hat and downplay the insurance gig. If my experience in Green Haven held true up the coast, law enforcement would not be welcomed with open arms in what I assumed was another self-sufficient, self-sustaining "we take care of our own problems" kind of town. If I was there to help organize the search for Parker Alley and gained trust and access from and to certain key people, I was confident that I could avenge the death of Jason by bringing real justice. I wasn't really concerned with whether Parker had killed himself or not. My feelings after this morning's conversation with Audrey resurfaced. Cauterizing the artery that carried heroin to the extremities was not what I had in mind. Stopping the heart from pumping was.

The road wound around and up and down through cleared acres, the centers of which were marked with farmhouses—Cape Cod–architectured, clapboarded homes with brick chimneys. Nearly all of the inhabited properties were dotted with small outbuildings. Barns, outhouses, woodsheds, and lean-tos displayed an array of roofing material and pitches. Between homesteads were forests of evergreens and clusters of hardwoods whose wet leaves clung to branches that swayed in the gusty wind. The only anomaly in the picturesque vista was the yellow road sign with a black deer symbol cautioning drivers to beware. The sign was riddled with bullet holes. I hoped the shots came from a frustrated hunter and were not indicative of a violent citizenry.

Farther along was an open field strewn with boulders; erratic rocks stranded by the melting of the last glacial period. Patches of low scrubby growth I knew were blueberry bushes lay in black charcoal, freshly burned. Doused in the rain, the scorched ground wafted a stale Cuban cigar smell, which was blown into my car by the fan. A sharp bend in the road led to another farm with its own fragrance. Split-rail fences surrounded muddy-looking pastures from which black-and-white cows barely noticed me as they chewed. These were livestock farms; there was an absence of cropland. Too many rocks and ledges, I thought as I crested the long gradual hill I'd been climbing for miles.

The view from the top of the hill, even in the miserable weather, was so incredible that I stopped in the middle of the road to gaze out into Cobscook Bay. The line connecting gray sky and water was made distinguishable only by the whitecaps on the bay. From this distance, it looked like someone had shaken a paint brush out on a drop cloth. Miami's shore, all skyline and sandy beaches, could never be seen from anything natural higher than sea level. South Florida and eastern Maine elicited such different feels, different weaves of fabric altogether, that it was dumbfounding to think that they were bookends harnessing the Atlantic Seaboard. The town of Cobble Harbor must be on the eastern side of the next hill below me, I thought. Never had the differences in my old and new home states been as poignant as they were right here and now, with farms tucked into hillsides behind me and the ocean sprawling below. Sad to think that heroin was a link in common. I had my work cut out for me, I knew. Treading on brand-new turf would require new techniques and rules. Cobble Harbor would have no crack houses to storm or corner coke whores to shake for information.

On the horizon, from my vantage point, rose an island out of the ocean. All round and smooth like a polished stone, Acadia Island appeared more inviting than it did when seen from Green Haven. I'd get there before the snow flies, I vowed as I looked in my rearview mirror to ensure that I was not holding up traffic. With no one in sight in either direction, I could have stayed. But I had duties to perform.

Continuing down the road that twisted around hills like a vine on a trellis, I forced myself out of the passive meandering I had been enjoying for nearly two hours into a more alert consciousness. The road I drove dead-ended at a stop sign marking a T intersection. Although there was no sign, my sense of direction and trip to Cobble Harbor by water yesterday pointed to the left. Soon I was on what I would call Main Street. The faded yellow paint line separating two lanes of traffic disappeared as the road narrowed between large stately-looking houses on either side. Nearly all of the houses were white with black trim and shutters. Many homes were crowned with a widow's walk, the small perch on top of the roof from which wives of sea captains could look out over the bay when husbands were expected home from voyages. This was the Maine you read about.

After a long row of pristine houses with picket fences, there were a number of small businesses, indicating that I was getting close to the waterfront. Restaurants, shops, antiques, a dentist . . . all advertised with tastefully designed and neatly painted wooden signs. I now understood the expression "hanging out a shingle." It dawned on me that I hadn't seen a single human. Hell, I hadn't even seen a dog. The businesses had lights on inside, so they were open. Perhaps everyone was at Jason Alley's funeral. It was gloomy. The weather and the funeral would probably limit the number of protesters, I thought. There would always be a few diehards who lived and preached principles while everyone else went about their business, believing but not acting. Between buildings on the right side of the road, I could see glimpses of water. But I couldn't find a road to get to it. Finally, just when I was searching for a good place to turn around and try the other direction, I saw a road marked with a sign that read PUBLIC LANDING—FISH PIER. I couldn't imagine anyplace else where Cobble Harbor dyed-in-the-wools could stage a protest or launch a boat blockade. I made the turn and hoped to find someone on the pier I could ask. I took a deep breath and realized that I was about to raise the curtain for Act I of a remake of an old show starring me.

The gate that protected the pier was connected to huge metal buildings for boat storage. As I entered the gate and passed the buildings, I saw that the menfolk of Cobble Harbor were all present and accounted for. I had it wrong. Blue lights flashed on top of state police cars and uniformed officers with megaphones paced the aisle squished between two agitated swarms of men. The curtain was up. Did I make my entrance, or wait in the wings?

6

OKAY, MAYBE THAT WAS a little dramatic. But in the spirit of "everything is relative," I must admit that I was taken aback by the scene as it was *so* different from what I had expected to find at a peaceful demonstration in Cobble Harbor, Maine, on a dismal day. Measured against other civil unrest I had witnessed, the place was not exactly crawling with cops. There were two cruisers, both with lights flashing as stated, and four officers—one of whom had a megaphone. The crowd was not an angry mob—more like an upset group. From what I could see, there were two sides engaged in what, even from my sealed car, sounded like a heated discussion. There wasn't a chance I would sit this one out. With so many people assembled in one place who might be on the verge of emotional outbursts and the disclosure of information they would otherwise have kept private, this might provide a real break. Discourse fueled by the heat of the moment might include useful information. Maybe I would gain a clue or two toward my investigations into vandalism, Parker Alley, and (if I was really lucky) Cobble Harbor's drug connection. I found a place to park, secured my holster, donned my rain gear, pocketed my badge, and headed for the center of the fray.

I approached the group slowly, intending to blend into the outskirts and listen until I had learned enough to make my presence known. I again looked over the crowd. Strangely, a few of the men were dressed in suits and long raincoats and wore Dick Tracy hats. They didn't look like cops but they sure weren't dressed like fishermen. Perhaps there was more going on here than the small ruckus I had been promised. Before I got close enough to blend, one of the state police officers saw me coming and slipped away from his post. Positioning himself directly in my path, he planted his feet and crossed his arms at his chest. "May I help you?" he asked.

"Actually, I'm here to help *you*," I said as I took a step to the side so that I could see the other men. He shifted over in front of me, forcing my attention to his face, which clearly depicted his attitude. It wasn't at all threatening. But he was giving me the look I had come to think of as a Maine thing. Not all, but most of the Mainers I had met were so suspicious of me upon first sight that I came to feel, in their eyes, as if I were a snake-oil salesman. I could almost see new acquaintances squeezing tight their wallets in protection. Maine would not be fertile ground for scam artists, I thought.

"You brought muffins and coffee?" he asked with a smile. His uniform pants were so wet they clung to his shins. The circle of men behind him was loosening. The party was breaking up. I had arrived too late.

I dragged my badge from my back pocket, held it up briefly, and shoved it back in. "No muffins. Sorry." I stuck out my hand to offer a shake. He accepted politely and his expression bore an apology for what could have been considered a chauvinistic remark. My skin had grown so thick over the years that nothing fazed me. Confidence and competence speak much louder than screams of discrimination. "Jane Bunker. I'm with the Knox County Sheriff's Department. I got a call about a blockade protest and came to see that everyone behaves. I'm really surprised to see state police here," I said, hoping for a reply that might answer my real question: *What the hell are you doing here?*

"Everyone is surprised. No one more than us. We never tread on counties' territory. It takes an act of Congress to get staties to respond to namby-pamby stuff like this. No offense. My guess is that a senator called the department. When deep pockets get worried, heads turn, and we get the nod. Know what I mean?" I really didn't have any idea what the officer was talking about, although I enjoyed the fact that he seemed to feel the need to justify his presence to me in what he assumed to be my turf. The guys behind him were dispersing. I recognized one of the dark-suit-and-trench-coat men, but couldn't quite place him. "Looks like we'll be out of your hair soon." The officer gave a glum nod to the man I thought I recognized as he passed. "All these guys want is to scatter a few ashes on the water; at-sea burial, I guess you'd call it. Now that we've discouraged the blockade, I think it's safe for them to go about their memorial service for that kid." A sudden gust of wind sent a chill through me as I realized that the familiar face was that of Parker Alley's brother, whom I had met yesterday.

"Heroin in Cobble Harbor. . . . Can you believe it?"
I asked.

"Don't take it personally. That shit is showing up everywhere. You've got as good a chance of stopping that as you do finding the kid's old man," he said. I would have loved to contradict him by informing him that I intended to do both, but kept my cards close and hoped for more insight. "Talk about a needle in a haystack. It's a big ocean. That's why I didn't join the Coast Guard. These guys on the *Quest*"—the officer jerked a thumb over his right shoulder toward the public dock—"they're conceited enough to *guarantee* they'll find the body if it's there. Some guarantee. *If* it's there. So, if they come up empty, they claim the body wasn't there, right? Hey, maybe they'll hire a psychic!" The officer laughed.

I joined him with a smile as an attempt to firm up my membership in the Maine law enforcement club. "I thought the research vessel was in town to do a survey for an aquaculture company. Now they're talking about towing for Parker Alley?" I asked.

"Yep, that's my understanding. The captain offered to do a search, hoping that would get him through the blockade unscathed. We were briefed, and I mean brief. The local fishermen are split on aquaculture, the Indians are mostly against it, reps from shipping companies that transport up the river here are fighting it. . . . The plastic company has yet to enter the ring. Hey, these are *your* people. You tell *me* how it unravels. In the meantime, let's hope that your fishermen stay aboard their boats. That would keep us staties from returning to this godforsaken outpost." The tone of this implied to me that the staties believed foul play might be a factor in the disappearance of Parker Alley. Though maybe I was reading too much into it. Or, more likely, he was. It would take something far more daunting than a bunch of fishermen barricading their home port and a possible knuckle sandwich to get state troopers to travel this far from their usual beat. Before I could ask, the officer's partner was beckoning him to get into the cruiser. "Brrr." The man shivered visibly as a drop of rain fell from the end of his nose. "We're heading back to civilization now." I assumed he meant some town north of Route 1. "I'll bet you even have a Grange hall here. Do you?" He was in the car before I could tell him that I didn't know.

Intrigued with who the deep pockets were and why they had sicced the state police on Cobble Harbor, I approached the only man remaining in the pier's parking lot. Someone had to fill in the blanks for me. Now that what had looked like an impending debate had been averted, and there was no need for me to think about jumping into the middle of a confrontation, I saw no reason to act as an authority or official of any kind. I could just be Jane Bunker. Civilians are more prone to chat with visitors or tourists than with the police. Yup, I would just be Jane Bunker from Green Haven. Maine locals also have great suspicion of anyone "from away," which is how they refer to those not born and bred in their state.

The man, who looked like a block of granite, must have heard me coming up behind him. He turned quickly, with his hands raised and curled in loose fists at his chin. "Whoa," I said as I fell back a step, creating a safety zone between me and this man whose nose appeared to have been broken several times. He lowered his hands slowly, closed his eyes, and exhaled a huge sigh that I took as one of relief that he hadn't flattened an innocent woman. His physique was impressive. Even in heavy, ill-fitting foul-weather gear, his body was an almost perfect rectangle. Not much of a neck, and a flattop hairdo made it impossible for me not to think of the cartoon character Sponge-Bob SquarePants. When he opened his eyes he hung his head in shame, shaking it slightly. Placing his right hand over his heart, he tapped his chest repeatedly and mumbled something that could have been a prayer, but could just as easily have been cursing me for startling him. This tough guy was a wreck, I thought. I had to let him off the hook. "I often get that reaction from men. But usually not this early in the relationship."

My words had the desired effect. He looked directly at me. His eyes were deep brown and liquid. He smiled, and I felt the sun. He began with an apology in a voice that contradicted my first impression of a nightclub bouncer gone to seed. Soft-spoken and articulate, his accent was a strange combination of Down East and clipped guttural. He was, he said, George Paul—one of the tribal chiefs of the Passamaquoddy Indians. If I hadn't been so immediately taken with him, I would surely have come up with a wisecrack regarding his name and half of the Beatles. But I was bowled over by him; not in a smitten sort of way, just impressed. He struck me as genuine and kind. George Paul seemed delighted to have someone listen as he talked, which he did. Unprompted, George Paul launched into an explanation of who his people were, what their situation was, and how they stood on all the issues most hotly debated in the state. He was open and honest, insisting that his people had nothing to hide, nor anything to be ashamed of. The more he talked, the more questions I had for him. He was thorough and thoughtful in answering them. Maybe a little too thorough, I thought, as he hit the fifteen-minute mark of a soliloquy in response to the question I should have asked first, namely: "What's going on here?" It had finally occurred to me that George Paul knew a lot about a lot— and the fact that he was so willing to talk was a great gift.

George Paul had begun his explanation in some year B.C. Still, he was so passionate and interesting that I barely noticed the activity aboard *Quest* behind him. He had my almost full attention as he gave the time line of the history of Native Americans in this part of the world; and when his narrative approached the present date, he did tie in the reason for his being in the parking lot. Although the information he gave didn't shed any light whatsoever on the questions I had about who was bringing heroin into the area, he did provide background I thought might ultimately be helpful to me in the performance of my day jobs. I had been sent here to keep the peace and to assist in finding a missing person and, perhaps, to determine if Parker Alley had committed suicide or, in light of what the state cop had implied, been done in. Anything I could gather from George Paul might be useful to those ends.

The first evidence of human life in this area, George Paul said, was in the Maritime Archaic period, when there were Red Paint People, so called for the large amounts of red ocher interred with their dead; tools from that era showed stains of similar red. Archaeological digs in shell heaps provided evidence that the Red Paint People hunted swordfish, which, according to a very proud George Paul, was evidence of sophisticated hunting and seafaring skills. "They were a progressive group. They went well beyond picking shellfish from the shore." Most of George Paul's ancestors were presumed wiped out in a series of tsunamis at a time when the ocean was rising and earthquakes were common. This jibed with the information that I had been told by Quasar yesterday, I realized. Just as George Paul was explaining the genealogical connection between the remaining Red Paint People and the "natives" first encountered by European explorers, I caught a glimpse of Dane Stevens, the handsome captain, as he paced the *Quest*'s work deck. I got briefly distracted as I tried to figure out how best to greet the captain so that he would want me to remain in his company after the greeting. When I turned my attention back to George Paul, he had advanced to the Abnaki and Etchemin divisions of the Algonquin nation.

What was not just fascinating but relevant to my tasks at hand was that George Paul was explaining the case for Indians having exclusive rights to a wide area of sea and seabed, including where the aquaculture farm was to go. George Paul told me that the Etchemins were seagoing peoples, and so were the Passamaquoddy, his own tribe.

(George Paul was no ordinary member, he added—he was the chief.) Passamaquoddy, he explained, means "People Who Spear Pollock." The Passamaquoddy fished up and down the river, but always pitched their base camps on the east side, where, he was quick to point out, we now stood. The Etchemins inhabited the west. Prior to 1820, when Maine became a state, treaties were signed between Native Americans and the Commonwealth of Massachusetts, and included the "grant" of plots of land that would become reservations; one such plot was Pleasant Point, where George Paul had lived since he was born. George Paul had been fishing since the age of eight—sixty years. He didn't look it, so I remarked on how well preserved he was. He took the compliment in stride, never wavering from the topic. Although the Supreme Court had given Native Americans tribal sovereignty, George Paul's opinion was that it hadn't amounted to anything significant. My new friend ran down the list of rights his people were being denied; behind him, a parade of lobster boats was leaving the harbor. As uniform as a string of pearls, the boats slowly filed out through the channel—a sobering funeral procession. George Paul continued. I couldn't help but be distracted as my eyes and thoughts followed the train of mourners.

George Paul fervently believed that his tribe of Passamaquoddy should enjoy the right to harvest from the ocean as they saw fit, unencumbered by federal and state rules. I admired his conviction and courage. I found remarkable his ability to speak so passionately, and yet without anger, about all the ways his people had been wronged. This was not a rant. But I knew his cause was futile. Too much time had passed and too many foes were arrayed against him. When he pointed to a bird that soared high above and said that the osprey needed no license to feed itself, I felt the need to steer George Paul to the meat of what I wanted, and away from his haunting and romantic plea for a return to the way that things were, the way he felt they should now be.

"Did you know Parker Alley?" I asked, more or less out of the blue. I had given up trying to find a good segue.

"I knew of him, yes." Then silence. Maybe I would get somewhere, I thought. The loquacious chief was suddenly a man of few words.

"Well, what did you know of him?"

"Off the record?" he asked, making me wonder what record he thought I might be keeping.

"Of course."

"He was their ringleader. . . . The Alley family couldn't make a move without his okay. That's the way it is around here with all of us. We look to someone to guide us, but Parker Alley was a bad man. He and his family have been brutal about keeping others out of what they consider their own private fishing grounds, which happen to be the most productive for lobster and also where North Atlantic Shell Farms are proposing to lease from the state. He was spearheading the challenge to the oyster farm proposal."

"Rallying a few dozen fishermen is not going to stop big business," I said.

"There's more behind him than fishermen. Shipping oil and cargo is big business, too. And Pine Tree Plastics will be put out of business if aquaculture gets a foothold. They've been polluting the river for decades. Toxic algae blooms caused by their discharges run right through my community. They've decimated the plant and fish life that once sustained us. It's part of aquaculture's appeal to the green world—they'll be responsible for forcing Pine Tree Plastics to adhere to regulations. 'Plastic' is a dirty word these days. Must be quite a quandary for the Greenies," he chuckled. "Aquaculture is no bargain, either." The sky grew suddenly darker and the rain was swept horizontally in the wind. I wanted to ask George Paul what he knew of Jason Alley, but suspected that, because of his age, he wouldn't offer anything useful. Thunder rumbled in the distance. It was getting difficult to hear him when the wind gusted.

Just as I was getting ready to excuse myself to head for shelter, a pickup truck pulled into the parking lot. "There's my ride," George Paul said. "Do you need me to sign a release or something?"

"A release? For what?" I thought that I had probably misheard.

"I assumed you might need my permission to quote me in your article. You didn't even take any notes. I'm impressed!"

"I'm sorry. You obviously have me confused with someone else. I'm not a reporter," I said with a bit of embarrassment, as I wondered briefly if I had inadvertently misrepresented myself. I was fairly sure that I hadn't. "It was nice speaking with you, though."

George Paul laughed—I assumed at his own mistake. "Another dress rehearsal! Figures!" Now the driver of the truck honked the horn to hasten George Paul's goodbye. "We never get any good press. Remember the casino referendum? November fourth, 2003, is forever etched in my memory as Black Tuesday. The best economic development plan Maine has had in a century, and even Governor Baldacci renounced it. We couldn't get the papers to talk to us so we never got to make our case." Another blast from the truck's horn got his attention. He thanked me for listening and turned toward his impatient ride.

The fact that he had mistaken my identity was useful in that it resulted in his providing me essential background and a glimpse into the intricately woven fabric of the Cobble Harbor community. I wondered how long George Paul would have lingered in the inclement weather had he not been trying to get his story into print. Nice accidental ploy, I thought. Now I needed to get out of the squall that was rapidly approaching. Rain I could handle, but I always felt uneasy in an electrical storm with a hunk of metal strapped to my midsection. I didn't want to give new meaning to the phrase "packing heat."

The two figures aboard *Quest*, which I had been observing intermittently since I had first stepped out of my car, had reappeared on the back deck of the boat. They were now appropriately attired in rain suits. The bright yellow forms were hunched over and appeared to be working on some kind of a project. The forms grew and gained contour as I neared; they finally looked human as I hustled across the aluminum gangplank and landed on the deck with a hollow thud. Both men looked up from their work. Smiles from beneath hoods were welcoming. Even with the hood ties limiting the portions of face exposed, I could easily distinguish the two as Quasar the scientist and Dane Stevens the captain. As I knew they were not expecting me, and I, too, had a hood cinched tight, I felt a reintroduction was in order. "Hi! It's Jane Bunker, from yesterday. The insurance lady, remember?" Before either man could speak, a flash of lightning lit up the sky and a sharp crack of thunder loud enough to split atoms shook us all to attention. Simultaneously, the men dropped shiny chrome tools at their feet and beckoned me to follow them into the fo'c'sle.

I scurried behind them through the open door and to the ship's galley, where a teakettle spat at the cast-iron stove, forming tiny puddles that hissed and then vanished, leaving behind a fine rusty residue. The captain secured the door behind me, cutting off the sounds of the storm that was now full upon us. My fingers were so numb from the cold I could barely find the loose end of my hood string. When I did, and pulled it, a thin stream of water was squeezed from the knot and ran across the heel of my hand and up my sleeve, one of the only parts of me that had, until then, remained dry. The men removed their jackets. I followed suit, exposing a four-inch-wide dark stripe along the front of my sweater where the zipper had not even pretended to be watertight. "So much for the state-issued rain gear," I said softly.

"Cup of tea, anyone? Miss Bunker? Tea? How about a hot cup of tea?" asked Quasar in his nervous way, as he opened a cupboard and pulled out an assortment of teas from Red Rose to exotics that smelled like sweet pipe tobacco.

"Thanks. I would love one." I slid onto a bench seat across from Dane Stevens, who, with a hand gesture, invited me to sit.

"I see that you met Chief One Big Loon today," Dane said with a playful grin.

"Dane! That's so disrespectful," admonished Quasar from the counter, where he prepared three cups of tea. "He has a name. And you know it. It's George Paul. Don't be rude."

"Maybe. But he *is* crazy." Dane circled an index finger around his ear, the schoolyard symbol for "loopy" and something I hadn't seen anyone do since, oh, third grade.

"You are a bigot. You truly are a bigot."

"All I'm saying is that he's a nut."

"He's eccentric," Quasar corrected.

"Okay, you win," Dane said with a smile that showed off impeccable dental work or good genes. "But, if there was a Wal-Mart in town, they'd be missing a shopping cart." I really wanted to laugh at this, but Quasar hadn't. I certainly had not regarded George Paul as a lunatic, and had to consider the possibility that these two men were putting on an act to discredit something they assumed he said to me.

Quasar served the tea with a quart container of non-dairy creamer and a plastic bear of honey—a contrast to the fine teacups I was surprised to see aboard a boat. "I assume that FedEx found Cobble Harbor," I said as I pulled the hat off the plastic bear and squeezed a spoonful of honey from the hole in the top of his head.

"Yes, they did. They did indeed," Quasar said as he removed his steamed-up glasses and rubbed them back and forth on his shirt front; the lenses rattled as they crossed buttons. The extent of his squint indicated that he was probably legally blind without the aid of eyeglasses. He pushed the glasses back on, forcing the ear-pieces through the tight mass of red curls, and opened his eyes, seemingly delighted to have regained his sight. "Yes, FedEx delivered late yesterday afternoon. We're nearly done fixing the damaged equipment."

What followed was a long awkward silence. The three of us sat sipping tea, smiling at one another, and each of us wondered whose turn it was to say something next. I was certain that it was not mine, and I couldn't for the life of me think of anything intelligent, witty, or interesting to say. Even sarcasm had abandoned me. So we sat quietly sipping for quite a while before I thought I noticed the men sharing a strange look. As soon as they saw I had noticed, they severed eye contact and concentrated on their teacups again. The next time I caught them sending signals across the table, I gave Quasar my patented "What?" look, which no one could misinterpret. But just to make sure, I raised my hands and pulled my neck into my shoulders. "Are you going to tell her?" Quasar asked.

Dane nodded. "I talked with your boss," he said, raising his gorgeous black eyebrows and waiting for my reaction to a statement I was accustomed to hearing just prior to the filing of a formal complaint about my investigation methods.

Don't get defensive yet, I warned myself. "Which one?" I asked.

"The Knox County sheriff."

So, now the men knew I was not just the insurance gal, which was fine. "And?"

"Well, I didn't know he was your boss until I called," Dane said, sort of apologetically. "When the state police left, we got worried about what could happen if the fishermen regrouped. Quasar and I both think that the vandals were trying to keep us from doing the survey that's needed for the leasing of ocean floor from the state. That didn't stop us, so they planned the blockade. There must have been a leak or a tip-off, and now the blockade has been foiled. We're not locals. We've heard stories about how these people treat their *neighbors,* so we can only imagine how they would treat people from another part of the country." Again, there was a pause. He hadn't said anything that required me to respond, so I didn't. The captain looked at the scientist for reassurance, which came in the form of a coaxing head nod. He began anew, this time speaking faster. "The cops said we should contact the County Sheriff's Department as this kind of problem is more in line with what they—or you, I guess as it turns out—would handle." Dane stirred his tea relentlessly as Quasar nodded his head in agreement to everything he had said. "The sheriff said he had already given you a heads-up and that you should be here. And here you are."

"Here I am. Everything is copacetic. I don't plan to leave until I get to the bottom of a few things, so I'll be around." I had actually intended to return to Green Haven fairly soon after the boats involved in the memorial service had been secured back to moorings, and after I had the chance to offer condolences, and, in the process, connect with some members of the Alley family. If timing and the stars lined up just right, I figured I could then get the information from those family members that I would need to begin my investigation into the source of illegal drugs in the region. Best-case scenario was a meeting with Parker Alley's wife, I thought. Connect, go home, return . . . that was the original plan. But I could hang a bit longer if Dane Stevens and Quasar felt my presence was necessary or made them more comfortable.

"Actually, the conversation turned from our equipment to the subject of that poor missing fisherman. What your boss said was that going offshore with us to find his body was entirely within your jurisdiction and duties," Quasar blurted out. That took me by surprise, but didn't stun me. I just didn't see it coming. "North Atlantic Shell Farms is okay with us recovering the body if it's within our survey plot." I swallowed and thought for a few seconds, formulating a response that wouldn't sound negative. Quasar continued: "Your boss wants you to call him. Do you have a cell phone? Cell phones work here. They work fine. There's a tower on Swan's Island. Or you could borrow mine. It works great."

Dane Stevens dug in his pocket and fished out a crumpled scrap of paper. "Here's the eight-hundred number, in case you don't have it on you," he said, and handed me what looked like the edge of an envelope. "Here, use my phone." I would have preferred to make the call in private, but knowing what was behind the door for weather, I decided to remain right by the stove. I was prepared for the answering service to say that no one was available to take the call and advise me to leave a message or call 911 should it be an emergency, but when the beep sounded for the message, I hung up without leaving one.

"There's nobody available to take a call. When do we leave?" I asked, intentionally including myself in the trip. Now that I had a minute to digest the idea, I realized that it was a good one. Both of my bosses would be satisfied, I thought.

"As soon as this weather passes, which could be right about now." Dane Stevens got up to look outside. "Let's cast off. Quasar, you can finish the magnetometer on the way to the site, right?"

"Yes. Yes, indeed. It won't take but a few more minutes." Quasar stood and pulled his yellow slicker back on.

"I wasn't planning to go, but that's fine," I said, re-solved to do the right thing concerning both of my jobs. "When will we be back ashore?"

"As soon as we have a dead body or a completed bottom survey, whichever comes first." The captain disappeared out the door, saying he had to fire up the engines while Quasar secured the galley for departure.

"Don't worry," said Quasar. "We can't stay offshore for more than seventy-two hours. It's written in our contract. If we want to stay longer, we need to hire crew, and we can't afford employees—tight budget. In fact, if you weren't going, we would have only forty-eight hours. It's an insurance thing. I guess you understand that!"

I was being shanghaied, I thought. I was the nonpaid crew member who was buying them an extra twenty-four hours to do their job. I hoped that I was being paranoid and that Dane and Quasar really felt that I was needed in some way that related to my insurance or law enforcement jobs. But if the speed at which the ship was made ready to go was an indication, they were nervous that I would come to my senses and bail out before the lines were thrown. What the hell, I had had worse duties, I thought. Much worse. I could always make the best of any situation, I knew. I followed Quasar onto the deck, where the sun was now shining brightly. I was reminded of a saying I had recently heard: If you don't like the weather in Maine, wait a minute.

I assured Quasar that I could handle the bow and aft spring lines, and carefully walked the narrow rail around the wheelhouse to the foredeck. Out in the channel I could see the boats making their way back into port. At least the sun had come out for their homecoming. Cremation is nice and neat, and either useful or terrible if it later turns out that an autopsy is needed. Several times during my stint working homicide I had been frustrated by a cremation. By the time an autopsy was ordered, the body was already toast and the crumbs had been sprinkled in the wind. Oops.

"Let 'em go," called Dane Stevens, referring to the lines he was now ready to see cast free of the pilings. Quasar and I coiled and stowed the sections of braided nylon while the captain slowly maneuvered *Quest* away from the wharf and toward the buoys marking the north end of the narrow channel. The wind had switched to northwest with the passing of the low pressure system; steep waves, working against the incoming tide, crashed onto the man-made, rocky breakwater whose purpose was to protect the inner harbor from storm surge. Chilled from spending so much time in the rain and wind, I sat for a minute to soak up some of the sunshine and allow my rain gear to dry out in the stiff breeze. The inlet looked rough enough to send spray onto the bow, so I headed for the shelter of the bridge.

"May I borrow your phone again?" I asked the captain, who stood behind a huge spoked wheel. Impressed with the range and number of electronics and computer monitors, I thought it would be fun to learn about some of this high-tech equipment, and began looking forward to getting to work. The captain handed me the phone without a word. I could see that he was concentrating on navigating, so I stepped out the open door on the lee side of the house to make a call to my landlords, the Vickersons, to let them know I wouldn't be home tonight. In the sun and sheltered from the wind, I was happy and comfortable. I would connect with some representative of the Alley family soon enough, I thought. It might actually be better to wait. I sat on the foredeck with my back pressed against a bulkhead and dialed the phone. I was relieved to get the Vickersons' machine and thus not be stuck in conversation and interrogated about my whereabouts. I left a brief message. I closed my eyes to enjoy the warmth and thought I would remain here until we were out of the narrows and onto smooth water, and then I would join Quasar on deck.

I braced my feet and pushed my back harder against the steel bulkhead as *Quest* began rolling from side to side in increasing swells. Deep rolls turned to sudden pitching and slatting as we crawled by the breakwater that lined the west side of the channel. It would be rough for only another minute or two, I thought, as I gazed beyond the rocks spewing spray, out to where the surface glistened like polished silver.

A crash on our port side and a lurch toward the rocks felt like quite a heavy wave had caught us broadside, but when it was followed by a loud "What the fuck?" from the wheelhouse, I jumped to my feet and scrambled inside to see what the problem was. Something was obviously terribly wrong. Dane Stevens looked more than worried as he pushed the throttles up to full ahead and turned the wheel to the left, putting the rudder hard to port. I glanced out the windows on our port side to see the top of a boat.

I hurried across the wheelhouse for a better look at what was happening. A lobster boat had its stem against our port bow and was pushing us rapidly toward the breakwater. Even though *Quest* was at full power, we were losing ground quickly. Quasar came in from the work deck and screamed, "Oh my God! What's he doing?"

"He's forcing us onto the rocks, and there's not a fuckin' thing I can do about it." Dane held the wheel hard to port, eased the throttle, and shifted into reverse in what I supposed was a desperate attempt to let the lobster boat slip by our bow. It was no use; this resulted only in increasing our speed toward the breakwater as the lobster boat persisted in propelling us closer to where the violent surf pounded. Dane put the engine back in full-speed-ahead mode, and we watched the distance to the menacing shore grow smaller still. "Quasar! Get the survival suits!" The scientist was paralyzed with fear. He didn't budge, and it didn't matter, I thought. There wasn't time to climb into the clumsy survival gear. I knew I had to do something fast, or we would be pummeled against the breakwater until the ship broke up and sank. "Quasar! Come on, snap out of it! Fifty-four-degree water!" This time the captain had shouted even louder at his friend, who still was unable to move.

That did it for me. I tore my gun from its holster and charged out onto the foredeck, where I was nearly face-to-face with a dark figure behind a windshield glaring from the sun. The other boat was truly right upon us, like some kind of demon. Aiming to the right of the figure at the helm, I squeezed off a shot that blew a hole in the Plexiglas the size of a nickel. Shifting my bead to the left, I hesitated before firing again. But the warning shot had done the trick. The lobster boat that had been driving us into the rocks suddenly drew away. And as she turned, I caught the name on her stern: *Spartacus*.

7

I WATCHED *SPARTACUS* over the top of my gun and kept the sights trained on the middle of the driver's back until I was certain that he had no intention of having another go at us. He never glanced back, so I didn't get a look at his face. A police sketch rendered from my eyewitness account would bring in most of Cobble Harbor for the perp walk: adult male, average height and weight, wearing orange foul-weather gear—useless. But, I thought, as I lowered my gun and secured it back in its holster, I did have the name of the boat. One phone call would give me the name of its owner. And tracking down a person by name had always been infinitely preferable to going door-to-door with a fuzzy picture. I took a deep breath and contemplated how effortless firing the shot had been—like second nature. Slinging a gun was a knee-jerk reaction born of good training and bad experience. Chalk another one up for the latter. I gripped the handrail and peered down into the water, preparing for reentry into the wheelhouse. What would the men think of their new shipmate—a modern-day Annie Oakley with sensible shoes?

I could see the bottom down below the scarce few feet of water we were in—jagged rock and ledge that have the ability to tear open the hull of a steel boat like a can of sardines. Good thing this old tub of a vessel didn't have a deep draft, I thought. The way *Quest* rolled nonstop suggested that she had a fairly round bottom and didn't require much water to float, and the fact that we weren't sinking was a better indication yet. I watched the harbor's floor fade and disappear in the increased depth as Dane found the center of the channel again. Far behind us I could see several segments of the funeral procession landing at docks and moorings, and I wondered whether *Spartacus* had been part of the service or had just found it convenient to tag along, hoping for an opportunity to pounce. My investigation into the identity of our attacker would, of course, need to be put on hold until I was back on terra firma. And that would be sometime in the next three days. I waited outside the bridge an extra minute to allow Dane Stevens time to get squared away as I assumed this episode was far enough out of his comfort zone to warrant it. I waited another minute to fully recover from the physical aspects of my fight-or-flight reaction. I needed to transition back to my more casual and less primal self.

When I felt fully composed, I stepped into the wheelhouse and latched the door behind me. The captain was busy increasing the range of the radar, putting a waypoint in the GPS track plotter, and getting the autopilot set up. Quasar, who appeared to be in shock, stood gripping the edge of the forward console panel and staring wide-eyed at the horizon. Rather than pretend that someone hadn't just posed a serious threat to our lives, I decided to remind the two that I was, in fact, in law enforcement and was not simply to serve as their crew member. Yes, Dane Stevens was our captain. And yes, Quasar was our scientist. But I had something of value to offer, too, and had clearly already proven myself to be more than just their ticket for an extra twenty-four hours offshore or someone to put a pot of coffee on the stove. "What do you know about the *Spartacus*?" I asked, intending the question for both men. Neither answered. "Anything?" I hoped to get something of a reply, even if it was a flat "No." When Dane finally pulled his face out of the radar, he shook his head and frowned. "Have you ever seen that boat before?" I kept asking questions but wasn't getting much in return.

Again Dane shook his head. When I forced eye contact, he said, "No. I don't remember ever seeing it. But there are so many lobster boats in Cobble Harbor that it's hard to place one specific boat."

"How about you, Quasar?" I asked, trying to shake him out of his trancelike state. I placed a hand on his shoulder and asked again, "Quasar? *Spartacus*? Any recollection?"

"Yes, of course," he answered, seemingly pulling something from his memory. The captain and I waited as Quasar rubbed his chin in concentration. I was holding my breath in anticipation as Quasar slowly emerged from subconsciousness. He tapped his right temple with an index finger, then opened his eyes wide in an *aha* expression. "The movie was released in the early sixties. It starred Kirk Douglas." Dane rolled his eyes—either in amusement or exasperation or both. I was merely disappointed. I had thought for a second Quasar was going to tell us something really useful. Quasar, unbowed, continued. "What a story. And based on fact! Spartacus was captured after deserting the Roman army and was made a slave. The biggest and strongest slaves, like Spartacus, were sent to school to become gladiators. Watching fights was the Romans' favorite form of entertainment—quite the barbaric sport. Spartacus led the slaves in a revolt against the Roman Empire in what we now know as the Servile War." I was relieved that Quasar was not showing any signs of classic shock. He was speaking coherently, albeit about something totally irrelevant. Interesting how Quasar's speech lost the nervous repetition when he was reciting fact from memory. "At the top of his game, Spartacus had one hundred and twenty thousand followers. They raised havoc for a couple of years, but were finally defeated by forces led by Crassus. It's believed that Spartacus died engaged in battle in southern Italy, but his body was never found. As an interesting aside, Pompey—"

"Quasar, shut up. That's not funny," Dane interrupted.

"It wasn't meant to be funny. I was answering Ms. Bunker's question. And if you weren't so rude, you might learn something," Quasar scolded.

"Our bodies could be smashed to bits against the breakwater right now if Jane hadn't fired her gun and convinced that guy that the next bullet was going right into his head, and you're giving a lecture on ancient Rome." Quasar hung his head slightly and pouted like a child who had been reprimanded. The captain, aware that he had hurt his friend's feelings, softened his tone as he continued. "Look Quas, if you have something pertinent to say, please do. If not, why don't you get to work on the gear? We'll be on-site in thirty minutes. We haven't given up on that bonus yet, have we?"

"Right. I'm going. I'm going," Quasar replied. "We have a bonus to collect. A bonus. Let's just pretend that didn't happen back there." Quasar moved toward the door slowly, talking as he went, supposedly to himself, yet just loud enough for Dane and me to hear every word. "Pertinent, what could be *more* pertinent? What I was *trying* to get to before I was so rudely interrupted was what Spartacus represents. It's the classic struggle: good versus evil, oppressed versus oppressors, peasants versus aristocracy. The good people of Cobble Harbor think we're the bad guys. No wonder we're under attack. . . ." And his voice trailed away and faded into silence as he disappeared around the corner. I was relieved to hear the mention of a bonus, which I assumed was some financial reward for meeting a schedule. The quicker, the better, I thought.

Alone for the first time with the attractive captain, I hoped I would not revert to the idiocy I had come to expect from myself whenever I found myself in the company of a potential suitor. Suitor? I hated myself for the thought! And I also hated myself for using, even in my head, such a weird old-fashioned word. Why do I become like some Jane Austen character the minute I start to fancy someone? The absence of a ring on his finger and the fact that he had just referred to me by my first name had led me to premature, immature castles-in-the-sky musing about whether he found me at all enchanting. That I had never been described in that way before did nothing to keep me from hoping that he was, right now, in *his* head, applying that very word to me. It was just a few short months ago, I reminded myself, that I had had a near miss in a love connection with Green Haven's most eligible bachelor. My role in sending his brother to prison hadn't done much to get our relationship out of the blocks, I knew. My brand of "justice above all" had fouled every good relationship I had ever almost had, but my dismal record never stopped me from trying to start new ones.

"Good ol' Quas. He's a very sympathetic guy," explained Dane, as if he felt the need to apologize for his friend. "Sometimes his feelings make it hard for him to make wise business decisions. He can be very irritating. I'm sorry. He makes me insane most of the time."

"Why do you continue to work with him?" I asked, glad to be drawn out of my fantasies. (Though I couldn't help smiling when it occurred to me how cute it would be to be part of a couple called Dane and Jane.)

Without any hesitation, Dane looked me square in the eye and said, "Because he's the best there is. I guaranteed the Alley family we'd come back with a body. And we will. We will because Quasar never misses. He's a genius. The only problem is that the genius has a conscience and acute sense of social justice. He's ready to back out of this project. I can tell. The only reason he's aboard now is to find closure for the grieving family." Then, as an after-thought, he added, "Well, that, and the fact that he wouldn't leave me holding the bag. We were college roommates, so we've been butting heads for a long time. We'll survive Cobble Harbor and be off to our next contract. I guess you could say he's my best friend, even if he drives me crazy."

Well, maybe I was a better match for a guy like Quasar, I thought. Smart, good at what he does, a real sense of what's right, and he follows his convictions . . . Too bad he's so funny-looking, I thought. No, too bad I'm so shallow. Dane continued. "He's brilliant, really. I've yet to stump him on any topic. Even Spartacus . . ." Oh no, my worst nightmare was coming to life. The object of my budding romantic interest was interested in me only as a possible mate for his nerdy best pal. I had to stop him before he got to the part about what a wonderful father Quasar would make.

The thought of giving birth to little Quasars did not appeal to me. What if they were girls? Little Quasar girls. "So, we don't yet know who tried to run us ashore," I said, scrambling for the safety of a comfortable topic. "But we do have plenty of people with motive."

"Yeah. It's becoming clear that there is a lot of opposition to this aquaculture project. People can get pretty emotional when they come up against new enterprises. Progress is the enemy, you know? They see change as dumping on their heritage, and in a place like Cobble Harbor heritage is worshipped like a god." I knew this was true. I had experienced the identical situation in

Green Haven with a proposed wind farm. But, I thought, it wasn't quite as simple as Dane suggested. There were folks like George Paul, whom I had just met, who would embrace some change, like a casino. There are always two sides, and sometimes three.

Quest was sliding along easily in the calm water; the gently rolling waves provided a slight, shallow dip from port to starboard and back, just like a hand on a cradle. The sloshing sound of her blunt bow, plowing rather than cutting a path, was a peaceful accompaniment to the tranquillity all around. The captain covered his mouth with a hand to conceal a huge, silent yawn that I hoped was due to the temporary lull and not indicative of the quality of my company. "Oh, excuse me," he said. "I'll go put on a pot of coffee if you're okay keeping a lookout for a few minutes." Impressed that he had not suggested that I make the coffee, I happily volunteered to do so, saying that I needed to learn my way around the boat. I asked to borrow his phone again, as mine was in my car, and he gladly lent it.

As I stepped out, I admired the way the sun had transformed the day so completely. Harbor seals stared, their heads like pears sculpted in black marble, and then quickly dropped beneath the surface as if through a trapdoor, leaving behind concentric rings of ripples. A night or two at sea in these conditions would be delightful, I thought. It had been years since I had had the pleasure of darkness offshore. Well, I had spent some time hiding in a bilge this past June, I reminded myself. But this would be different. This would be like old times fishing with

Archie in the Gulf Stream, when we would go offshore far enough to escape any trace of the bright city. Arch would douse the deck lights, and we'd sit on the fish hold hatch, dangling our legs and marveling at the greatest show on Earth. He'd be up for parole in another year. He'd been framed. Though I couldn't prove it.

The clanging of steel on steel from a wrench dropped on deck shook me from my thoughts and brought me back to the mission at hand. I made a quick call to the Sheriff's Department to request they run a check on *Spartacus* and learned that the folks of Cobble Harbor are a bit more sophisticated in their criminal activity than I had imagined. The boat had been reported stolen just a few short hours ago by its owner, Willard Kelley, the tipsy pilot Cal and I had taken ashore from the *Asprella*. Buyer's remorse; I wish I hadn't bought into this trip now that there was a concrete lead and a place to begin my investigation ashore. Too late, I thought. I would just have to make the best of it. On the other hand, I realized if I hadn't made the trip then I wouldn't have been aboard to witness the ramming and get the lead. So it was all evening out.

An open can of Maxwell House was in the cupboard directly above the automatic drip machine. Secured to the bulkhead with a bungee cord, Mr. Coffee appeared to be safe in any sea conditions. I knew from my various fishing experiences that caffeine is one of the two most important ingredients for maintaining crew morale—the other being nicotine. Of course, bountiful catches and great weather help, too, but since these aren't sold at any chandlery, smart cooks stock up on java and butts. I dumped coffee into a paper filter and filled the pot with water from the tap at the galley sink, both in amounts to make a full, strong pot.

After pushing the button to start the brewing, I walked the length of the gangway toward the bow, opening doors as I went. Three double staterooms and a large bathroom with head and shower completed the tour. The stateroom closest to the bow appeared to be unoccupied, so I assumed that was where I'd lay my head when the time came. I hadn't had any warning, so of course I had no pillow or sleeping bag. Hell, I had no clothes—not even a toothbrush. I had been in worse places with less, I thought, as I closed the door and went back to the galley to check on the coffee. The machine was working, but ever so slowly. Rather than stand and watch, I joined Quasar on the work deck. "How's it coming?" I asked as I approached.

"All done! Just finished! A lot of the damage was superficial. We're in business now. We're good to go. I'm just waiting for the captain to give me the word that we're on-site and I'm ready to get this show on the road."

"Dane is very confident that you'll find the body of Parker Alley. Do you search for bodies often?" I asked. Why did I phrase it that way? I worried that my question sounded like a cheesy pickup line. I turned away from Quasar and inspected a hydraulic winch that appeared to be used to launch the ROV (remotely operated vehicle).

"Most of our work is in surveying bottom and doing water-quality tests. We measure and chart tide, current, and salinity, and note sea life—stuff like that. We get a lot of jobs through the Army Corps of Engineers. When someone applies for a permit to build a dock or dredge a channel, we put in a bid for the survey."

"But you have done searches for missing people, haven't you?"

"Oh yes. We have been hired to find drowning victims, and we've been quite successful. Very successful, in fact. Eight for eight. Perfect score."

I relaxed with this information. "Wow, Dane said you were good. One hundred percent success rate on eight assignments? Here's hoping for number nine." I crossed my fingers.

"Of course, two of the victims were trapped in a plane that went down off Cape Hatteras. That was an easy one. But still, we've had seven successful missions of this type. I shouldn't take much of the credit. It's the captain's expertise in narrowing the field of search. I'm just the technician. Dane is the man. He's very well respected in the world of oceanography, marine biology, and marine salvage. He may come off as a bit gruff, but his bark is worse than his bite. He's a great guy, really. I've known him for a long time. He's a wonderful friend, and . . ." Oh no, I thought. This can't be happening. The nerd isn't the slightest bit interested in me. He's talking up his friend. If it wasn't so depressing, I'd have to laugh. At least I wouldn't have to worry about locking my stateroom door tonight.

"Coffee?" I asked. Quasar wasn't ready for caffeine just yet, he said, but he was certain that Dane would love a cup, black. So I left him on deck surrounded by his machinery to bring coffee to the bridge. After delivering to the captain and returning his cell phone, I was sent by strong suggestion back down to the deck, where I might be useful to Quasar when it came time to launch the ROV. I wasn't there five minutes when Quasar thought of a reason to send me topside again. Before I could hop to it, I felt the boat slow to an idle. Dane joined us on deck and saved me the humiliation of watching him conjure up another task requiring me to be with his friend.

"We're close to the first track line. I'll give you a hand with the side scanner first," Dane said as he twisted the valve on the hydraulic motor that controlled a large winch wrapped full of half-inch-diameter cable. The motor turned slowly, backing wire off the spool until there was a loop of slack on the deck. Dane turned the motor off and joined Quasar in the stern, where he was untying something that looked like a miniature submarine that was attached to the end of the cable. Both men eased the towfish, or "fish" as they called it, out of its bracket and rested it on the rail. "Jane, could you operate the winch?" Without answering, I grasped the brass handle that I had just observed Dane using. "Inboard is up. Please take up the slack until the fish is hanging from that bollard," Dane said as he motioned to a large block over his right shoulder. I did as he requested, twisting the valve open until the winch moved, slowly wrapping the slack wire back onto the spool until the wire was tight enough to pull the fish off the rail and hold it under the block.

"Perfect. I'll give you the word to lower the fish into the water. We want to tow at twenty fathoms, Quas."

Dane quickly vanished back into the wheelhouse, leaving Quasar and me at the winch to wait for his command. "What does the towfish do?" I asked. Quasar, as I had already learned, enjoyed explaining things about the equipment and engaging in any kind of chat that bore no resemblance to normal conversation. He quickly gave a description that I knew represented his best attempt at using layman's terms, but he still seemed to be struggling with dumbing it down sufficiently for me to understand. I learned that the fish was the housing unit for a side-scan sonar, one of three machines in *Quest*'s acoustic imaging system. The fish was designed to "swim" as it was towed at different depths through the water behind the vessel. Similar to the depth sounder, which shoots an acoustic pulse straight down from a transducer on the ship's hull, a side scanner sends pulses across the seabed, covering a wider swath in each pass or along each track line. Pulses strike the seabed and are reflected back to the vessel, where they are received by the transducer and converted to an electrical signal, which is traced on a paper chart recorder and analyzed by the technician. The depth sounder is used to determine the depth of water under the boat so that the operator knows when to lower or raise the towfish.

Track lines, Quasar explained, were adjacent and parallel imaginary lines that covered the search area. Dane had already determined the area and the distance between the lines to be tracked, so we were about to engage in a systematic search. He'd figured out with the Coast Guard about search parameters for Parker Alley using information from the electronics aboard *Eva B.* Flawless navigation made possible by GPS meant that *Quest* would not stray from the lines or leave gaps in the area to be searched. Fortunately, the area where it was believed they would be most likely to find Parker Alley's body over-lapped the area they had been hired to survey for North Atlantic Shell Farms; two birds, one stone—or, rather, one towfish.

"When do we get to use this other stuff?" I asked enthusiastically.

"It will take almost twenty-four hours to cover the area with the acoustic gear. Then we should go over it with the proton precession magnetometer. And, ideally, I would like to try a few passes with the sub-bottom pro-filer over any lines where there's an indication of ferrous materials."

"Oh" was all I could muster with the realization that I really was in this thing for three days. Dane called out for us to lower the fish, and Quasar explained that the wire was marked with spray paint at five-fathom intervals. So I would need to stop the winch when the fourth mark was at the block. He pointed out the brake and asked that I tighten it once the wire was towing the fish at the proper depth. I agreed that I could handle this job, and he ran to the bridge to watch the chart recorder for "anomalies."

Manning the winch, as it turned out, was fairly inac-tive duty. But it took me several hours to figure out that I did not need to stand with my hand on the brake, ready

to release it to change the depth of the towfish at a moment's notice. It was dark by the time I relaxed enough to
sit on a basket full of line up by the boat's exhaust stack,
which radiated enough heat to keep me warm well after
the sun went west. Every thirty minutes or so, the boat
would change direction, making sharp 180-degree
U-turns that batted the waxing gibbous moon back and
forth over the gallows frame that towered above the stern
deck. Boredom with what I was doing and curiosity
about what the men were doing finally got the best of me.
Under the guise of thoughtfulness, I barged into the
wheelhouse with a cup of coffee in each hand and a bag of
cookies under one arm.

The wheelhouse was dimly lit by electronics. Quasar
sat with his face pressed nearly against a machine that
was drawing a graph that resembled the feed out of a
heart monitor. "Hope I'm not interrupting anything," I
said as I looked for a spot to put down the coffees. I
headed for the light over the chart table, and Dane sprang
to his feet. He beat me to the table, closing an open book
and turning it over so that I could see only the back cover.
"Your brand of pornography?" I teased as I looked at the
picture of a sinking four-masted schooner that he appeared to have been embarrassed about me seeing.

"Yes, sort of," he laughed. "It's *Unfinished Voyages* by
John Perry Fish. It's a history of shipwrecks in the Northeast. I didn't know whether you were superstitious or not
and might regard it as a bad omen or evil talisman." Then
he laughed loudly and added, "After our encounter with
Spartacus, I guess I should have known that a book

wouldn't spook you." He removed the book from the table, motioned for me to set the cups down, and slid the volume into a magazine pocket on the side of his chair. "Oh, thanks. It's going to be a long night. Why don't you go lie down and get some sleep? We'll wake you if we need your help."

I know when I'm not wanted, and I realized pretty quickly that they really didn't want me staying up with or dating them. I said that I wasn't really tired but would try to get a nap. Quasar thanked me for the coffee without taking his eyes off the graph or his thumb off the remote sending unit button, which was harnessed to the plotter by a thin cord. These men were serious professionals doing their jobs, and I should leave them alone, I thought. But I wanted to contribute what I could. I doubted that I would fall asleep while others were working; it just isn't my style. But sensing their strong desire to see me retire for the evening, I vowed to try to stay out of their hair until daylight, when I would poke around the galley for something breakfastlike for the three of us.

Once settled in my stateroom, I rolled my rain pants up to serve as a pillow and covered my torso with my jacket. But I was nowhere near dozing. Upset that I was at sea, wasting time when I could be gathering information on the heroin trafficking, I tossed from side to side, fighting alertness while I assumed the men above waged war with drowsiness. Maybe I could do a shift for one of them. How much coffee could they consume before it no longer did the trick? I could certainly run a boat well enough to follow a line on a plotter. And I'm a quick

study. I could learn what to look for on the various monitors, and wake the men when I found something. They
could both sleep while I conducted the search. If I didn't
fall asleep soon, I would suggest that.

I must have fallen asleep at some point, since Quasar
woke me with a knock on my stateroom door. "Miss Bunker, are you awake?" The door opened a crack and Quasar spoke through the opening without looking in. "Miss
Bunker, are you awake?"

I hopped out of the bunk and opened the door the rest
of the way. "Yes, I'm awake. I couldn't sleep," I lied.
"What is it?"

"We've located something that could be your man. I
mean it might be. We're not sure, but it could be. I hate to
say probably, but more than likely. I'd be surprised if it's
not him. It's within a hundred feet of the exact center of
the area Dane scoped out for the search. Too much of a
coincidence to be a false alarm. . . . I hope it's him. Very
likely could be. We're preparing to tow a net over the spot
to see if we can scoop it up and thought you would want
to be on deck."

"I'm right behind you," I said as I followed Quasar
out onto the deck, where the sun was just rising. So I
had slept for a fair while, I realized.

The captain quickly explained what I needed to do to
help. First, we needed to retrieve the towfish and secure
it in its bracket, which we did. Next we would have to
make some adjustments to the net the men usually used
for "sea sampling"—that is, for seeing what kinds of fish
were swimming in a particular area, a survey require-

ment of the Department of Marine Resources. "We'll take up a couple of links on each end of the chain," Dane explained. "That will keep the net's lower jaw, if you will, from digging into the mud and rocks. If that's a body down there, we don't want to drag it along the bottom and then up to the surface with a bunch of rocks. It wouldn't be pretty." I didn't bother telling the men that I actually had vast experience with net adjustment after years aboard commercial fishing boats. I simply listened and did as I was told, and soon we were setting the net out over the stern. The net's configuration was one I had never seen before, towed from one wire instead of the usual two. I learned that it was a Skipper Drew design called an OLAK, which they said stood for "One Legged Ass Kicker." As I backed off the winch, lowering the net into the water, I hoped it would live up to its name this morning.

The captain returned to the nerve center of the operation, where I knew he would be concentrating on towing the net over the spot where he believed the body of Parker Alley lay. Quasar and I hung out on deck while the boat moved steadily toward the sun, which was now fully above the horizon. Soon the boat spun around and towed back in the opposite direction. "He always makes two passes, just to be sure," Quasar confided. "I suspect he had it on the first run, but there's no way of knowing. Some boats have cameras they can launch with the net and see everything that goes in, but we don't. That's why he makes the second pass. Just in case. The net cameras are expensive. It's a lot cheaper to make a second pass.

Parker Alley is probably already in the net, but without the camera, there's no way to know for sure." Quasar was fidgeting nervously.

"I thought most drowning victims were recovered by divers."

"We really aren't interested in making our livings pulling dead bodies out of the ocean. This is not what we like to do. Dead bodies are not our thing. North Atlantic Shell Farms thought this would help with public relations. And divers are expensive. We can't afford divers. We're a low-budget operation. We may need to hire some divers later depending on what the data of the survey shows. We have equipment. Do you dive? We have our own compressor to fill tanks. Are you certified?" I shook my head and stared over the stern at our wake. I prayed that Quasar was right about already having the body in the net. There were so many questions that I couldn't get answered until my feet hit shore, and I knew my impatience with this trip would grow exponentially. And Quasar's repetitions were starting to annoy me.

Quest's engine slowed to an idle, while my pulse sped up in anticipation. Dane arrived on deck and ordered me to release the winch's brake and begin to bring the net up. As I did so, the men stood on either side of the stern and looked aft. "Keep a slow, steady strain on the wire. That's a good speed," the captain said, then quickly watched the water behind the boat again. When the last mark approached the winch, I slowed the winch slightly, as I knew the net must be close to the stern now. I watched Dane as he pointed an index finger at the sky and drew a circle around and around, the signal I recognized as an order to keep the net coming up. When the finger dropped into the hand, making it a tight fist, I shut the valve off, stopping the winch from turning. "Now back off the boom winch. The valve is on the bulkhead behind you." I found the valve and followed his commands, going back and forth between the two valves, until the net had been disconnected from the tow wire and the mouth had been secured, by a hook, to the winch on the boom high above the stern deck.

"Okay, Jane, take it up slow." As the mouth of the net was pulled up, the webbing behind it followed up over the stern, until the very end of the funnel slid onto the deck and hung, swinging slightly, just a few feet in the air. "Bingo. Got him," Dane said, sounding quite relieved in spite of all of his confidence. I joined the men as Quasar gave the purse line, which cinched the end of the net, a quick jerk, popping open a clip that allowed Parker Alley to fall onto the deck like a dead fish. Although a dead man was precisely what we were expecting, we were all taken aback by the large steel rod that pierced his chest and what appeared to be blood or red paint on the side of his face and clothes.

8

MY SHIPMATES WERE INTENT on covering up the corpse as quickly as possible and so, in the absence of a proper body bag, produced a down-filled sleeping bag from within the fo'c'sle. This kind of sleep was probably not what L.L.Bean had intended for the users of their product, but Dane and Quasar had no qualms. I suspected that their haste to conceal Parker Alley was twofold. First of all, until you've seen a large number of dead strangers, the presence of a corpse is creepy and, as with the accident scene syndrome, compelling in a way that makes it difficult to remove your eyes. Unless you are conducting an investigation or an autopsy, there is some guilt involved in checking out a dead body. Out of sight, out of mind, I thought as the men gently lifted the body onto the open bag, placing it on its side so as not to disturb the steel, wooden-handled rod that ran completely through his upper abdomen, bayonet style. Second reason? Covering a dead body just seems the right thing to do and shows proper respect for the dead.

Quasar folded the navy blue, down-filled nylon over Parker Alley, and Dane operated the zipper that ran the length of the bag, miraculously, without a catch. I was still somewhat amazed that they had found Parker, and so very quickly. Either these guys are very good, or extremely lucky, I thought. I have always been somewhat relieved when things go according to plan, especially at sea. When Dane had casually mentioned the subject of superstition, I felt a bit of a pang of guilt; everyone knows that women are considered to be bad luck aboard a boat. Kindly, no one said anything. The thinking, or lack thereof, goes like this: When Lady Luck sets sail, she morphs into Jonah, and is held responsible for every bad thing that happens from foul weather to poor fishing to downright disaster. I've always been welcomed aboard boats, as I have learned that men like to have an excuse handy for when things go awry. Don't get me wrong: I have never been blamed for someone else's mistake, nor would I stand for that. Like Mother Nature, I have been held unjustly responsible only for the big stuff.

Accidental death was now a tough sell, I thought as I followed the men up to the bridge. Murder? There was no evidence of that. Parker Alley had been alone. And with so many boats working within radio or even visual contact, foul play was unlikely, I thought. Homicide would have to be ruled out. Suicide? Tough to fall chest-first onto a spike like that and then keel over into the water. But not impossible. If Parker Alley had indeed committed suicide in a grief-stricken or depressed state following the death of his young son, he certainly didn't take any chances on the success of his first swimming lesson. While hari-kari may have been considered an honorable death in some Eastern cultures, suicide in any form is shameful in ours. The only explanation I could imagine for Parker Alley's thoroughness in his self-destruction was, perhaps, his maritime heritage. Would it be considered an embarrassment for a fisherman to die with everyone thinking that he had accidentally fallen overboard? The amount of pride people take in their saltiness and seafaring abilities, nurtured over generations, could conceivably seduce someone on the brink to wish to leave no chance that people would think his death was caused by a misstep or incompetence. Better to show the world that this was quite intentional and remove all doubt of ineptitude. And yet how could he have been sure his body would be found? Maybe he just assumed as much.

The remains of what appeared to have been red paint, definitely not blood, formed a long smudge that ran the length of the corpse's left side and gave the indication that Parker Alley was right-handed. Otherwise he couldn't have painted the stripe on himself. Of course, I made the obvious connection to George Paul's history lesson, recalling the early Native American Red Paint People. But I couldn't figure out what kind of a statement Parker Alley was trying to make with the paint and it baffled me. Trying fully to understand the thoughts and intentions that would precipitate this kind of ultimate, violent self-destruction is often foolhardy, I know. But it's what I do.

People who haven't spent too much time around dead bodies are often reluctant to speak within their earshot, as if they could hear, and this was certainly the case aboard *Quest*. Nothing was said until we were all in the wheelhouse and the door had been secured. There was no real discussion, only a statement issued by the captain detailing our new course of action. He had decided that it would be best to steam to Southwest Harbor, where the nearest Coast Guard station was, and basically get rid of Parker Alley and me. He was almost that blunt. Keeping in mind our send-off from Cobble Harbor less than twenty-four hours ago, it seemed like a wise point of disembarkation for me, whether I was with or without a body. I was anxious to get ashore for many reasons and assumed that I could hire or hitch a ride to collect my car. So the captain got no argument from me.

I agreed to call the sheriff to report the recovery of the body and to have him inform the next of kin. My call was accepted, and I learned that the county coroner would also be notified, as protocol necessitated the corpse be officially pronounced dead prior to anyone removing it from the vessel. We were just two hours out of Southwest Harbor, so this seemed like a good plan.

I borrowed a sheet of paper and a pen from Quasar, as I had left mine in the Duster back in Cobble Harbor. The first thing I wrote down was "Bait Iron." Quasar, who was reading over my shoulder, questioned my notation. I informed him that this was the common term for the wooden-handled instrument with which the corpse was skewered. I recognized the rod as a bait iron, the kind used aboard many lobster boats to spear whole baitfish onto a line so that they could be held fast in the proper spot in a trap, and theorized that this one had been the personal property of Parker Alley. Next, I asked

Dane for the precise latitude and longitude where he had "caught" the body, for accurate paperwork and to check against the location where Cal and I had happened upon the abandoned boat two days ago. Other than noting date and time and the other facts, there wasn't a whole lot I could do in the line of duty until my feet hit the ground in Southwest Harbor. There was no urgent reason to call Mr. Dubois regarding what should be said to the underwriters of Parker Alley's life-insurance policy, and it shouldn't be done anyway until I had filed a proper police report. When you wear two hats, you have to make sure to remember which goes on first. The insurance folks would be the only people pleased to learn that accidental drowning had been ruled out. Parker Alley's last thoughts had certainly not included his widow's financial security. A simple jump into the water would have left open the possibility that his death would be ruled accidental and would have made it possible for her to collect.

The wheelhouse was uncomfortably quiet as the green puddle of landmass over the bow rose from the bay and took shape as if melting in reverse. "Is this detour going to screw up your bonus?" I asked, intentionally breaking the silence. Quasar seemed both surprised and ill at ease with my question about his compensation; I assumed that he'd forgotten that Dane had mentioned the bonus in front of me the day before, when he was trying to shake the scientist into action during the breakwater scare.

"I hope not," replied the captain. Then the men looked at each other with what I felt was a bit of distrust, as if they both suspected the other of having foolishly shared a confidence. With a slight shrug that could have been forgiveness or apathy, Dane continued with an explanation. "Aquaculture is a hot topic these days and there's a window of opportunity for public input. If North Atlantic Shell Farms can get their ducks in a row faster than the opposition can organize a fight, their chances of pushing the proposal through is good. Our data is a required part of the application for leasing the bottom from the State of Maine. Like most of our contracted work, there's a small bonus in completing the job by a certain date. We still have two days and the weather report is good. So, as long as we don't dally in Southwest Harbor, we could make it."

"Any bonus for desired results?" I asked.

"No," Dane replied in a tone that indicated that he had been asked the question before, perhaps posing it himself. "No money for shading data. North Atlantic has done their homework. They know that this area of Cobscook Bay has ideal growing conditions for oysters and that all variables that Quasar and I will measure and record will pass muster. Our work is a formality. The only obstacle to the proposal is the public's opinion of it."

"Well, so far it appears that at least some of the public is not on board to the project," I said with a chuckle.

"And fortunately, our paychecks do not hinge on the success of the proposal. It doesn't matter to us whether they grow oysters or not. That would only lead to suspicions that we fudge data. We're not about that." I believed him. Dane pushed a button on the autopilot, shutting it off, and began steering the boat by hand as we neared the first set of channel markers. Here were two nice-enough fellows trying to make an honest living, and struggling at that, finding themselves on the bottom floor of a contentious project, which made them into targets. Quasar had summarized the situation best in his Spartacus analogy. The residents of Cobble Harbor who opposed big business, or change, or aquaculture specifically, would naturally see Quasar and Dane as foot soldiers of "the bad guys," and Quasar was certainly justified in his feelings of being "under attack." All the more reason to be landing in neighboring Southwest Harbor. I wasn't finding any comfort in my vague recollection of ancient history. As I recalled, yes, Spartacus and his band of rebel slaves had indeed defeated many Roman soldiers against outstanding odds, but in the end he failed in his attempt to flee Italy and that failure had cost him his life. Of course, Quasar had that history down cold.

I was so wrapped up in thoughts of Spartacus and also figuring out how best to organize my time once we hit shore that I scarcely noticed the beauty of the day and the surroundings as Dane Stevens navigated a wide channel that led to a junction of intersecting waterways. Quasar had binoculars pressed against his eyeglasses. He scanned the shoreline back and forth with a slow, sweeping 180- degree arc. The captain spotted the Coast Guard station and had chosen the channel that would take us there long before Quasar pointed it out. Floating docks were connected to high piers that lined the shore all along the face of the brick buildings that housed the Coast Guard base. Two of the larger government vessels were tied to the pier, while a number of small boats hung on floats. The *Eva B.* was tethered alone to the farthest float in the compound, as if she'd been quarantined. Moorings were held by skiffs and dinghies, all of which appeared to have been left by the fishing fleet, as they lacked the Coast Guard color scheme that signified and glorified every other floating object in the area. A flagpole towering above all displayed the appropriate symbols of our location: U.S. Coast Guard Group, Southwest Harbor, Maine.

Young men and women dressed in dark blue uniforms were busy with scrapers, paintbrushes, and garden tools as they manicured buildings, boats, and grounds; they were carbon copies of one another from their necks down to, and including, pant legs that bloused above boot tops into which they were neatly tucked. Two men stopped what they were doing on an adjacent float and hustled to the pier where we were coming in so that they could help catch lines. They wore dark blue ball caps embroidered across the front with yellow block letters: U.S. COAST GUARD, each hat read, and included the official insignia. The men greeted us with serious nods. High tide and a perfect docking by our captain made line tossing easy for Quasar and me. The young men placed eye splices down over pilings, and Quasar and I took tight wraps with bitter ends of four lines around prospective cleats. Then all bustle stopped momentarily, a clear indication that word of *Quest*'s cargo had preceded our arrival.

"Thank you, gentlemen," Dane Stevens said as he emerged through the starboard wheelhouse door and down three steps onto the work deck. His thank-you was a dismissal, and the young Coast Guardsmen took it as such. They asked if there was anything they could do to assist and seemed relieved to hear that we were all set and just waiting for the coroner to show up. They tore their eyes from the sleeping bag and walked back up the pier and into a central grassy area. Once there, they were quickly joined by half a dozen others who were, no doubt, full of questions and wanted the advance team to confirm or deny the rumors they had all heard about a dead body. I found it strangely refreshing that a corpse in their general vicinity had the effect that it did. The young men and women were distracted from work and their constant watch on the station's entrance gate suggested that they were disturbed by the scene. How different, I thought, from Miami, where I had on occasion seen pedestrians step over a body lacking posture on a curb and never break stride or miss a sip of their Starbucks. "It might be a while before the coroner shows up," Dane said. "Do you see any reason for us to hang around? I mean, if you need us, we're happy to stay. But otherwise, time is really growing short. You'll be okay, right?"

"Well." I tried not to sound disappointed. "Well, the only problem is that we aren't supposed to move the body from the boat until there's an official death pronouncement." The three of us stood and stared at one another with expressions that spoke with some volume about how ridiculous that was. "Let's pretend I didn't say that. This has already been a huge inconvenience to you and, yes, I'll be fine waiting here. The tide is going to start ebbing soon. Help me with the body and I'll throw your lines." It felt better being in favor of what was inevitable. Plus, being a proactive, take-charge girl who was willing to bend the rules was more becoming than being a whining stickler, I thought as I lifted what I knew was the foot end of the corpse. The three of us set the bagged body onto the pier with ease. We all shook hands, bid thanks, and said farewells. Dane Stevens and I exchanged phone numbers at his request, something that I naturally read more into than the stated, obvious reason: I would almost certainly need to follow up with him on official matters relating to the corpse and investigation, and to complete paperwork, and his employer might need to reach me. As Quasar slackened lines, I lifted the looped ends from the pilings, freeing *Quest* to venture back offshore. "I'll return your sleeping bag to you," I called through the open door as the boat pulled away. I watched until I saw nothing but stern; I was like the girl left behind at the railroad station. Out like a lamb, I thought. My wistful hopes of romance dissipated, like a green, twinkling, outgoing tide over sandy shallows. "Bye," I mumbled. I looked down, and the sparkle-filled backdrop was gone. The lump in the blue bag brought reality screaming back into focus with some velocity.

My stomach growled. Other than a couple of Little Debbie snack cakes I had helped myself to from a box I found on the galley table, I hadn't eaten today. I couldn't in good conscience leave Parker Alley here while I looked for food. There must be a mess hall or commissary on the premises. I looked around at the buildings. Maybe some of the onlookers would find the courage to come close enough to say hello and ask if they could do anything for me. Maybe not, I thought, as the closest group of three turned away when I looked in their direction. I would just have to wait. I began walking up and down the pier, never more than fifty feet in either direction from Parker Alley. It wasn't a nervous back-and-forth pacing as much as it was a time-passing activity. I find that thoughts come easier to me while I'm doing something mindless, like walking or driving. And I had a lot of thinking to do.

I soon grew tired of pacing and thinking. I had basically run through every possible scenario that might explain what had transpired over the past two days, rehashed all forty-one years of my life, and come up with an entire self-improvement strategy by the time I decided to sit and rest on a short piling beside the corpse. My knee-high rubber boots were sock eaters, having chewed the white cotton that had hugged my calves and spit it out into the toes, where it cramped all five digits of each foot. Kicking off the boots, I retrieved and replaced my socks, then pulled the boots back on and began humming an Otis Redding tune. I was glad I didn't own a wristwatch. Even the Coast Guard had grown bored with the not-unfolding scene and everyone had resumed their various maintenance activities. By the time I had chirped through the whistling part of the song for about the fifteenth round, a black hearselike vehicle pulled slowly through the gate, followed by a large silver pickup truck. They had a leg up on Green Haven, I thought. At least they had a hearse instead of a converted bakery truck.

I stood and waited by the body while the hearse backed toward the end of the pier. When it was as close as it could get to where I stood, two men emerged, one from each side of the front seat. They nodded in my direction, and then waited for someone to climb out of the truck that had parked just ahead of them. The truck was a crew cab. The inside of the large cab appeared to be full of people whom I assumed were Alleys, since I recognized the man who was now shaking hands with the coroner as the brother of the deceased, the fellow I had originally met offshore with Cal, and the same person I had seen yesterday in Cobble Harbor dressed for the funeral. One of the men opened the back of the hearse and pulled a backboard type of stretcher from inside and carried it down the pier toward me. The other two men followed close behind.

Quick introductions confirmed the driver of the hearse was indeed the county coroner, whose job was to pronounce Parker Alley dead. The man with him was the Alleys' family doctor, who had agreed to issue a medical certificate of death by drowning to eliminate the postmortem examination and allow the family to get on with the closing of this horrid chapter. Obviously, they knew nothing of the spike. Maybe, though, they could still get away with saying death by drowning and not by suicide. Who knew what you could do in these small towns?

I learned that Parker's brother was named Evan Alley, as all three men introduced themselves to Knox County Deputy Sheriff Jane Bunker—that is, me. I warned Evan to prepare himself before the bag was opened. He said that he appreciated my concern, but he didn't believe anything could faze him at this point. He said that he was just a walking zombie and wanted to put this in the past for his entire family.

"Let's get to it," said the coroner as he knelt down beside the sleeping bag and began to work the zipper. He unzipped nearly the full length of the bag before finally unveiling the corpse with a quick peel of the sides of the bag.

Evan Alley's reaction was as I expected it might be, in spite of his initial calm and assurance that he was ready for anything. He gasped and the color drained from his face. He grabbed the front of his own shirt and beat it in and out as if trying to get air. He turned and began walking toward the truck. It must have been awful for him to see his brother's body, especially with a bait iron through it. But I was the one who was surprised when I heard what he was wailing. "It ain't him," he cried. "That body ain't him."

9

I DON'T STUN EASILY, but I felt as though someone had pulled a chair out from under me. If this was not Parker Alley, who was it? And where was Parker Alley? The coroner, doctor, and I stood speechlessly and watched the scene unfolding by the side of the pickup truck, from which the family had emerged. There were tears of what I imagined were extreme frustration and disbelief, and hugs of support. I wanted to introduce myself to the Alleys and set up a time to talk with Lillian, whom I assumed was the woman in the center of the group, the one who was now dabbing the corners of her eyes with a handkerchief. But I knew I should wait for at least a few minutes to allow them a bit of privacy as they absorbed this mixed news. How would it feel, I wondered, for a wife to be on the receiving end of a negative ID? Would there now exist a glimmer of hope that your husband was still alive? Or are your hopes of closure dashed in bitter disappointment?

I shifted my focus to the corpse. Funny, I hadn't thought to look at the man's face until now. In the brief time on the *Quest*'s deck before he was covered, I had concentrated on the means of death rather than the dead. Jet-black hair, a small mustache, and a slight slant in the shape of his eyes; he certainly didn't look like someone central casting would have sent over to play the part of a member of the Alley clan and resident of Cobble Harbor, Maine. I pried an eye open. It was as black as I had ever seen in someone living or dead. I checked the pockets of his jeans and denim shirt, hoping for some clue to his identity, but came up empty. Unzipping the foot end of the sleeping bag, I exposed black socks and black Nike sneakers. I patted down the corpse's legs—nothing. In my experience, anytime an adult male is found with absolutely nothing in his possession—no wallet, no cigarettes, and no loose change—it is because someone has handled the corpse before the cops. "Do you know who this is?" I asked the men.

Neither man had any idea of the identity of the corpse. "So much for the quick ID, death certificate, and ride to the funeral parlor," said the coroner. "Give me a hand loading him up, would you please? I'll drop the doc back at his office and head to the morgue in Augusta."

"Will there be an autopsy report available for me to see?" I asked.

"There will certainly be an inquest. We'll need statements from you and the captain of the vessel that recovered the body. Our budget doesn't allow for many full autopsies, but we'll do a clinical inspection with toxicology." He pulled his wallet from his back pocket and handed me a business card. "You can call my office in forty-eight hours to have a copy faxed to the Sheriff's Department. In the meantime, it looks as though you'll be busy finding a missing person and a murderer."

Murder, although it was quite obvious, was something that until now I had been hoping could be explained away. Now that the coroner had said the word, there was no denying that this probably could not have been a suicide. A murder investigation would certainly distract me from my goal of damming the flow of illegal drugs into my territory. Of course, this apparent murder could be related to drugs, I realized. But right now, until I had some very basic facts, I knew I shouldn't even be trying to make a connection. I had to think for a second about why I was so much more interested in solving the drug case than in finding a murderer. It wasn't that I couldn't get excited about helping to convict a killer—of course I could. But that would simply mean getting justice for someone who was, well, let's face it, already dead. If I was able to stop the heroin from coming in, I would be helping prevent future deaths.

"Before we zip him back up, I'd like to see if anyone can ID him," I said as I took a step toward the truck. When I got no objection, I turned away from the coroner to see the Alley family coming down the pier single file, with Evan in the lead. The coroner, doctor, and I fell into place quite naturally to shield the fully exposed corpse from view.

"Miss Bunker, this is some of the rest of my family. I thought you'd need to talk with them, and they all want to have a look at the body," Evan said, and then introduced the three other people to the coroner and me. They already seemed familiar with the doctor. The young man was Evan's son, as I had assumed upon seeing them together aboard *Ardency* at the scene of the circling boat two days before. The middle-aged man was another brother, Jack, the youngest of three Alley boys. Lillian was a striking woman with classic facial features—high cheekbones and skin that appeared to dislike the sun. Her green eyes were rimmed red; she looked like she had been crying straight through from when her son had died until now, and she held herself in a way that suggested she wasn't sure if her crying would ever end. When I extended my right hand to her for a shake, she grasped the outside of it with her left and gave it a tight squeeze, as her right hand was now holding her nephew's arm for support. "I warned her about the body," Evan said of Lillian. "But she wants to help if she can."

"I'm a big girl," Lillian said. "What can be worse than seeing your son in a casket? Besides, Parker and I have been married since we were kids. I know better than anyone who his friends and enemies are. If it's someone who knew Parker, I'll know who it is." The coroner and I separated, leaving a wide gap between us through which Lillian passed with her nephew. She released her grip on the young man's arm when they were next to the body and then she circled slowly, looking at him from every angle. After a few minutes, she carefully pulled the sleeping bag back over the top of the body. "I've never seen him, but that could be my husband's bait iron in his chest."

"Lillian, you don't *know* that," Evan said, sounding as if he were pleading with her not to say anything more.

"That's ridiculous. Every lobster boat on the coast of Maine has a tool just like that aboard. It could be mine."

"Look, Evan: Parker is missing; they searched for him and found this guy instead. This isn't New York Harbor, and these people aren't stupid." I refrained from thanking her for the compliment. "Parker is not a violent man, but he would defend himself." She was now addressing me specifically. "If he killed this guy, it was self-defense and he is still alive, right?" My opinion was that Lillian was grasping at any hope, but she could be delusional and actually believe that her husband would be home for dinner tonight. I knew from past experience that people clinging to hope, even to the remotest possibility, are always far more likely to talk than people who have come to terms with a loss. I needed to have some time with her before the last glimmer of optimism faded away. "Do you plan to continue looking for my husband, Ms. Bunker?"

"Indeed I do," I answered. "If your husband is alive, we need to move quickly. Missing persons who aren't located within the first seventy-two hours of their disappearance have a tendency to remain missing. I could get search warrants for your house and the boat, and can requisition your records, but that would waste precious time."

"How can we help?" Lillian was now enlisting her family members, who did not resist.

"I'll need access to everything—phone records, bank statements, financial portfolios, tax returns, receipts, personal computer, personal correspondence in any form—everything. I'll need a list and contact information of friends and enemies." So far all of this was met with eye contact and a nod to each item I mentioned. "I'll need to talk with anyone who may have seen Parker the day he disappeared." Lillian seemed genuinely interested in not only cooperating but participating in the investigation, as she pointed at Evan and let him know, in a loud whisper, that she expected him to be able to supply those names. Now, I thought, was the proper time to push my luck with Lillian. "And as painful as it might be for you, I will have to ask questions about your son." I genuinely felt bad about asking and opening up such a fresh wound, but my investigation into the drug problem also needed to move swiftly or any leads would probably evaporate.

Lillian grew about two inches in height due to the sudden tensing of every muscle in her body. I knew I had pushed too hard too soon. Sadness in her green eyes was replaced with anger as she said, "You'll leave Jason out of this, or you'll get no help from me." Like any mother, Lillian was naturally willing to throw anyone or anything under the bus to protect the memory of her child. I apologized and agreed to concentrate only on finding Parker—for now.

The men seemed uncomfortable, having just been faced with a situation that could have escalated to something very ugly, very quickly; they got busy putting the corpse into a real body bag and then placing the whole kit and kaboodle onto a litter and into the back of the hearse. While they did, I tried to distract Lillian and get her to forget her near rage with lists of things for her to do and information to gather. As long as we stayed on the subject of how to expedite my investigation into the whereabouts of Parker Alley, well, then we were fine. With what I knew so far—the circling boat, the absence of its captain, and the corpse with a bait iron through its chest, found just where a body would be if it fell off Parker's vessel—I had a hard time pretending that I might be looking for a missing person and not a murderer and/or another corpse. I recalled the message left by Mr. Dubois about changes to Parker Alley's life insurance policy and understood that such adjustments could indicate many things. But my search for the alive-and-well Parker Alley would give me cover as I charged into the innards of Cobble Harbor; I hoped the show would be worth the price of admission. And, although searching for missing persons is really more about paperwork than real investigating (now, busting drug rings—that's genuine detective work!), Parker Alley was my responsibility, alive or dead. I was, after all, deputy sheriff and insurance consultant.

By the time the door of the hearse was slammed shut, Lillian and I were speaking civilly and had agreed that she would get to work on her end as soon as she got home that afternoon. I was to meet her the following day at ten A.M., at her house, to which she gave me simple directions from the town dock. She climbed into the front passenger side of the truck as Jack took the driver's side and the nephew hopped into the backseat. My silent wondering as to where Evan would sit was answered after the truck left him behind in the parking area. "The Coast Guard has released Parker's boat, so I'll steam her home to Cobble Harbor," he explained.

"Can I catch a ride with you?" I asked, remembering that I needed to get to Cobble Harbor to pick up my car.

"My wife would not appreciate that. Sorry." He looked genuinely embarrassed to deny me the lift.

"Oh" was about all I could say to that. "Well, I will need to get aboard the *Eva B.* to take a look around for the insurance company," I added truthfully.

"Maybe you should catch a ride with the coroner. He has to go right by your car to take the doc back to work," Evan suggested. "I'll have the boat back home before you get there and will leave her tied at the town dock. You can go aboard and do whatever you need to do."

I had a suspicion that Evan didn't want me aboard his brother's boat for some reason other than a jealous wife, but the coroner and doctor were getting into the hearse, and I really needed a ride. I didn't imagine Southwest Harbor had taxi service. I had already been aboard the *Eva B.*, and she'd been at the Coast Guard station for nearly two days. So what would the harm be in waiting a couple more hours to do a thorough inspection? I chased the hearse as it slowly pulled away, catching it before the gate, and giving the Coast Guardsmen another scene to ponder.

The coroner and doctor talked freely in my presence, or I should say they talked across me as I sat between them on the bench-style front seat of the hearse. Although I had been willing to ride in back with the corpse, I was pleased when the doctor opened his door and offered me a place up front with the living. The coroner had begun the inquest and I was glad to hear what the Alleys' family doctor had to say about the clan; most of the Alleys were his patients. They were good people, in his opinion. Everyone was shocked by the death of Jason. In fact, his had been the first and only overdose from heroin or any other illegal substance in the area that the doctor knew of. Drugs had always been a factor in Bangor, which was far more metropolitan than the remote towns situated on the ends of these long, twisting peninsulas like the one we were now traveling, the doctor said. He knew of a few methadone clinics in Maine—in Bangor, South Portland, Waterville, and Westbrook—but everyone always said that no such clinic was needed in this vicinity. And until just recently, the doctor had believed that to be so: "The traditional belief was always that the drugs just never made it down here from Bangor. But with the traffic this area sees in the summer from every major city in the country, I guess it was only a matter of time." Interesting, I thought, that the summer community bore responsibility for the local drug trade in the doctor's eyes. "And now we've got a murderer on the loose. What next?"

The coroner asked more questions about the Alley family, but the doctor didn't seem to have much more to add. All he could say was that they seemed to be quite a healthy group, as they appeared only for scheduled yearly physicals. They didn't even smoke or drink, the doctor confided, and this was most unusual among the year-rounders who relied solely on lobster fishing for their livelihood. "Slow fishing drives most of them to drink, which they can't afford for all of the reasons we're aware of. The Alleys are good fishermen, and Parker is known all over town as top dog. I wouldn't say he's well liked, but that's common. You know, a jealousy thing." A little soft prodding by the coroner on the subject of enemies had the doctor admitting that, while he wasn't in the know enough to provide names other than "Beals," which echoed Quasar's opinion of a long-running family feud, he did understand that lobster fishing was a cut-throat business in which only those willing to cut throats survived. What he didn't say, but he clearly implied, was that Parker must have been plenty willing to cut throats to be known as the best.

The car grew quiet, leaving us with our individual thoughts. Mine focused mainly on the view of the town of Southwest Harbor through the car windows. Southwest is unlike Green Haven or Cobble Harbor in that it's a well-known tourist destination, as is Bar Harbor, which is on the same island as Southwest. And just about every-one on planet Earth who has heard of the State of Maine associates it with Bar Harbor, pronounced without the "r"s. Funny, I had never imagined a hearse traveling at greater than a turtle's pace. Through the years, I had been stuck directly behind the hearse in many a motor-cade for a fallen comrade and shudder to think that I actually complained about the lack of speed and looked at my wristwatch constantly. One of the vows I took when I left Miami was to deep-six the watch, which I had done with the idealistic notion that a timepiece would have no value if I had no schedule to keep. Little did I know that I would indeed have a schedule. But I would have had no trouble keeping it this afternoon. Someone was in a hurry. The doctor or the coroner—or maybe both.

From the inside of the hearse looking out, the surroundings seemed to be flashing by at great velocity. I noticed a number of inns and B and Bs, now restored to funky, retro antiquity, one of the signs of a flourishing gay community. I remembered when the same transformation took hold in South Beach. Defunct businesses and dilapidated buildings suddenly came to life with a definite flair and tastefulness that was not exclusive to the gay community, but certainly was a hallmark of it. Everything was beautiful until the place started attracting more and more of the fast-lane crowd. Yes, I thought, this was the way South Miami looked twenty years ago. I hoped that Southwest Harbor could stop the wheels of change right here, before the straight fashionistas moved in.

Happily, there wasn't any evidence of fashionistas yet. Plaid flannel billowed around bodies that had not been near a gym; bodies that paused in the doorways and parking lots of the small restaurants and gift shops that lined the road on the way out of town. The storefront windows of a boutique we passed did not display clinging synthetics designed to accentuate runway-ready figures. Nope: Denim, cotton, and wool were the fabrics on hand—practical, functional, comfortable—and "high-end, modest conservative" was yet again the look in vogue this season, and all of the store's mannequins were dressed accordingly. The people I saw were draped in and covered by, rather than poured into and scantily clad by, their clothes. The wardrobe boss in Southwest Harbor liked colors other than black.

At the heart of the town, the quintessential New England church stood with perfect posture, stark in its whiteness and with a pencil-sharp steeple that cast a long shadow; the tip of the shadow pointed directly to the small cemetery next door. My mother would have regarded that as a sign from God. Yes, I thought, we're all heading there whether we enter through the front doors or not. But some of us have work to do first. For a period in my life, my mother was a member of what I fondly referred to as "the religion of the month club." She'd dress my brother and me up in our best clothes and drag us to whatever institution promised that it would save us all. The first sermon in our new religion was always like spring for my mother: an awakening of possibilities. The next service was summer, in that we were all made aware of the hard work we had to do to save our souls, a kind of religious "make hay while the sun shines." Fall, also known as visit number three, found my mother disillusioned, and winter, visit four, brought total discontentment. Four visits each church—that was the routine. I knew it well. Fortunately my mother didn't believe in giving money to the church, because we never had any to spare—not even for Jesus. It was a shame my mother was never able to find what she was looking for. I watched the cemetery disappear down the right side of the hearse.

The coroner had turned on the car's radio, and we listened to the usual gung ho, over-the-top enthusiasm of a local announcer between sets of oldies. When we made a hard left turn off Route 1, I began to recognize the road. It was the one that led to Cobble Harbor; we were close to my disembarkation point. I was aware that the coroner was not from Cobble Harbor, and so assumed correctly that he wasn't familiar with local politics. So it was understandable that the coroner never asked the doctor his opinion of the aquaculture project's possible role in the disappearance of Parker and the murder of the unidentified man riding with us. Not wanting to step on the coroner's toes but eager to hear what the doctor thought, I interrupted America's "A Horse with No Name." (And how dare they put a song from the seventies on an oldies channel, anyway?) "What's your take on the oyster farm, Doc?"

"That's a real can of worms," he said. "My personal opinion is that it would be good to have some industry in town other than lobster, and most of us are opposed to going after more tourist traffic. But the fishing families, Anglo and Indian alike, are dead set against losing the area proposed. It's the only thing the Anglos and Indians agree on. They both see aquaculture as a step toward losing their heritage—part of which is the fight between them for fishing rights."

"Do you think either side is capable of murder?" I asked. There was that red paint on the corpse. And I again recalled George Paul's phrase "the Red Paint People."

"No. Gear wars have escalated in the past to the point of sabotage and threats, but no one has ever gotten physical beyond a punch in the nose. The proposed area for the oyster farm has been closed to fishing since the last battle over rights, because the state saw the potential for things to get out of hand. It was like two kids fighting over a toy—if you can't share, we'll take it away. Amazingly enough, both sides preferred that to dividing it equally."

"But what about the degree of anger over this particular project? I mean, sure, the fishermen will get only so violent when fighting with one another over who gets exclusive fishing rights, but don't people get way more riled in opposition to a force from the outside?"

"If you are asking whether I think the man behind us was killed in the battle over aquaculture, I have no idea. I can only tell you that he isn't a local. I'm the only doctor in town. If that man had lived in Cobble Harbor, I'd know him." The hearse pulled into the parking lot, where there were many cars and trucks, the Duster among them. The doctor held the door while I slid out, creepy sleeping bag in hand, and bid both men thanks and good-bye. They urged me to be in touch should I need any information I thought they could provide and drove off. My first move was to the Duster; I wanted to stow the sleeping bag and retrieve my cell phone and notebook. Once I had these things, I headed toward the dock, where I could see the *Eva B.* She was there just as Evan Alley had promised she'd be. As I walked, I stared at the cell phone's display screen, hoping for enough of a signal to call Dane Stevens and inform him that we were still missing Parker Alley's body. The appearance of three bars had me digging in my pocket for his number. The battery life indicator showed a deathbed's gasp worth of juice remaining. I dialed and hoped. When I got no answer, I left a message with the surprising news and asked for a callback. At least they would learn they needed to keep looking the minute Dane picked up his messages.

My first mission aboard the *Eva B.* was to find the bait iron. I searched the entire work space, but found nothing resembling a tool with which a man could spear a fish and thread it onto the bait line in a lobster trap. There was a chance it could be stowed below. I opened the door exposing the forward compartment. Empty, completely empty—not only was there no bait iron, there was also no sign of the abundant shipping supplies I had seen two days ago. Boxes, insulation, tape, labels—not there; even the cooler that held the gel packs was gone.

10

EITHER PARKER ALLEY WAS a neat freak, or some folks had gone out of their way to scrub every inch of his boat. Under the wash rails, where you can usually find some remnants of bait, blood, mud, or one of the many grassy seaweeds that come up from the bottom on lobster traps, the fiberglass looked fresh out of the mold. One of the first lessons I had learned in criminal investigation was not to let a big reverse faze me. Of course, I needed to remind myself of this throughout my career and now. The fact that the *Eva B.* had been either burglarized or cleaned up could be a clue itself that could help me solve the Parker Alley mystery—maybe even a more significant clue than any I might have found if nothing had been taken or scrubbed away. Suddenly, I had the chilling feeling that someone was watching me. Possibly paranoia, I thought as I went about my business. Another lesson I had learned long ago was never to let on that you are aware of being watched. I put the eerie sensation of being seen through binoculars out of my head, and hoped that whatever surveillance device was trained on me—if any— was not the crosshaired sighting mechanism of a gun.

It was hard to believe that someone could have come aboard right under the Coast Guard's nose without being noticed and steal stacks of white, insulated FedEx boxes and all of the accompanying supplies. Although there was the possibility that brother Evan had taken the missing supplies for his personal use, or had the thought to begin emptying the boat knowing that Lillian would be putting it on the market, it just didn't seem likely; I guessed, rather, that they had been jettisoned for some reason en route from Southwest to Cobble Harbor. It's a strange and unexplainable personal quirk, but when I think I am being watched, I guard my thoughts closely as if the surveillance could penetrate my skull and read my mind. Again, reminding myself of how foolish this was, I continued in both thought and action. It wasn't like I had uncovered anything yet that should make me nervous. But the sensation of being watched from afar was enough to make me keep studying the boat. Why would someone be watching if nothing on the craft was suspect?

It's traditionally the stern man's job to clean up the boat, I thought, as I lifted hatches and inspected compartments. And the stern man is quite often the son or daughter of the captain. I wondered whether Jason had been fishing with his father right before he overdosed. And I wondered if anyone was with Parker the day he disappeared. Everyone, including Cal and me, had assumed that Parker had been alone aboard his boat. But I'm not sure why we all assumed that. Certainly if anyone else had been aboard, they would have been reported missing, too. The doctor was of the opinion that Parker was the high-liner in the area, but that would be impossible unless he frequently had help. I knew from my varied experience aboard commercial boats that top producers have top-notch help, and no one lobstering alone, no matter how good, can keep pace with a good two-man team. Keeping this in mind, I assumed that Parker Alley would usually have at least one stern man, and may have even employed two to keep up a rapid pace with the traps coming aboard and the lobsters to be measured and banded. Although I hadn't done a thorough inspection of the *Eva B.* when Cal put me aboard the other day, Cal had pointed out that she was too clean to have been hauling traps when the fisherman went missing. I had been so emotionally invested in the possibility that a man might be struggling for his life, and so flabbergasted that no one appeared to be concerned, that I scarcely took note of the condition of the boat.

The parts of the *Eva B.* that showed signs of fishing activity—the plates of the hydraulic hauler that pinch the line between them as it turns, the block through which the line travels from the water to the hauler, and the hauling patch, which is a thick piece of fiberglass on the hull where the traps sometimes bump when they are hauled from the surface—all appeared to have some wear. But, I thought, not enough to suggest that Parker Alley was a hard-charger and top producer. Productivity is always a function of a combination of factors, the most important of which is effort. The more traps a man hauls, the more lobsters he will catch. There are the old-school guys who will claim to fish smarter, and catch more pounds per trap, than the men who just bull through the gear—hauling and dumping, as they say. But at the end of the season, it's always the guys who handle the greatest number of traps who come out on top financially, in spite of bigger overhead. I knew that the majority of the inshore fleet worked a season that ran from May through December, so if that schedule held in Cobble Harbor, it stood to reason that Parker Alley was not fresh out of the boatyard but well into the season. I couldn't say exactly what was amiss, but felt that things didn't add up. The major thing bothering me was the too-clean boat.

By the time I had surveyed the engine compartment, steering gear, rudder post, through-hull fittings, bilges, battery connections, stuffing box, bilge pump, alarms, twelve- volt electrical system, fuel manifold, and engine exhaust, my suspicion that someone had done a destroy-the-evidence bleaching had dwindled. It was clear that Parker maintained his boat to the nth degree. Grease fittings were wiped clean, the bilge sparkled, and the battery terminals were immaculate. The tools were well organized and wrenches gleamed; even the grease gun, which in every boat I've ever been on causes you to shudder before you grab it, was spotless. Anyone who kept a clean grease gun would certainly not allow blood or bait to remain in any corner or crevice. If someone had come aboard to steal things for resale, they would certainly have taken tools and left shipping supplies behind, I thought. A little disappointed not to find a smoking gun, I had to admit that I normally tended to read too much into everything. Perhaps I was even imagining being watched. If I was here doing a straight survey for insurance, and not looking for clues, I might not feel as though someone were spying on me.

The *Eva B.*'s safety equipment was more than adequate and beyond the legal minimum standards. Two portable chemical fire extinguishers were in good serviceable condition and inspection tags were up to date. Four life jackets and two survival/immersion suits were USCG approved and in excellent condition. The Coast Guard–required ring buoy, properly marked with the vessel's name and strips of reflective tape, was hung with a neatly coiled piece of braided line that was secured with a fisherman's bend to the orange life ring, ready to heave to a man overboard. Visual distress signals (flares and orange smoke) were stowed in a watertight box, and the first-aid kit was first rate. Check, check, check, I thought as I went through the surveyor's list. Parker Alley was, indeed, a neat freak. By the looks of all the safety gear and first-aid items, he had in mind to stay alive in the face of any problems that might come his way while offshore. As I walked to my car, I couldn't help thinking about Jason Alley and wondering about Parker's state of mind following his son's death. I also couldn't help thinking that the sensation of being the subject of surveillance was stronger now, as if I were closer to the source.

Thoughts of father and son occupied me all the way to Ellsworth, where I drove the Duster for gas. Sure, I thought, as I pumped fuel worth its weight in gold into the dusty tank, the loss of a child has to be horrifically tough—it's ruined many a person and destroys most marriages faced with it. But I had never seen it result in suicide, if that's what this was. I have handled more cases involving the death of a child than I can count, and the parents were always wrecked. You'd expect nothing less. But I always had a sense that they would find some way to go on with some semblance of their lives. And I think that most of them did. I'm sure that there were suicides later; but I never saw one within the first week. Were family ties that much stronger here? Was premature death that much more unusual here than in Miami? But why would that matter? When it's your son or your daughter, what do statistics mean to you?

I went back and forth and back and forth in my mind from what I knew, but just didn't see Parker Alley taking his own life from grief. I wanted very badly to connect death of son and subsequent disappearance of father, but couldn't build a theory on so few facts and such scarce evidence. The only concrete things I had were an OD'd kid, an unidentified corpse, and a missing fisherman. Still, a son and father perishing in such a short time frame: There had to be some connection. I've never bought stock in coincidence, and I couldn't buy it now.

As I turned south and headed down the homestretch for Green Haven, I made a mental list of what I needed to do the next day. I did have a few things to follow up on that could lead somewhere. Perhaps the medical examiner's office would have an ID sooner than the coroner anticipated. That would be my first call, I thought. I had an appointment with Lillian Alley that I was most looking forward to. Mother of dead son and wife of missing man—Lillian was my most important contact. I needed to call or track down Willard Kelley to ask about the report of his stolen boat, *Spartacus*. I hoped that I would hear from Dane Stevens regarding the message I left on his phone, but if I didn't, I would have to get in touch with him even if it meant using the Coast Guard to radio him. I would need to call Cal tonight when I got home to see if he would be available to taxi me aboard *Sea Pigeon* back to Cobble Harbor. This last thought came when I glanced at the fuel gauge and wished I had sprung for another gallon or two.

Dusk bloomed slow and high in the sky, and fell like a dark curtain onto a horizon that finally lost its red glow of footlights as the curtain met the stage. I have always loved this time of day. Not quite dark enough for headlights; everything was soft, but would soon stiffen into a sludge that could not be penetrated without them. My favorite hour is celebrated each and every day in Key West, I recalled. Mallory Square saluted every sunset in grand style—tourists would come from far and near to watch the sun go down, the same sun that they could observe from their homes for free. Key West had cornered the market on sunset and it was a thriving business. True Mainers don't celebrate the end of daylight. They're more inclined to appreciate sun*rise*. Switching on the lights, I realized that the days were indeed getting shorter and knew that the decreased daylight cut into the lobstermen's profits—as it's illegal to haul traps after dark. Yes, fishermen must curse this time of day.

I could see headlights at a distance behind me in the rearview mirror. They seemed to be gaining on me at a

rapid clip. I drove slowly, since the road was so winding
and still relatively unfamiliar to me. I had heard the locals complaining of "summer drivers" who held them up
by observing the speed limit, and sped up a bit as it was
clear that the driver of the truck now on my bumper was
impatient. I vowed to register the Duster and get Maine
plates before venturing out of town again. The driver
followed ridiculously close; I imagined that he was irritated and cursing the out-of-stater in front of him. I
increased my speed to fifty-five—ten miles an hour over
the posted limit. Still the lights were too close to my bumper for my comfort. At sixty-five miles per hour, I was
getting nervous. Probably a couple of teenagers feeling
their oats, I thought. I had heard the screeching of tires
night after night on the hill outside my apartment and
had seen the swirling black rubber street art. I pressed
the accelerator to the floor when I was on a straightaway.
The lights in my mirror went to high, nearly blinding me.
I was unable to increase the space between the two bumpers as I approached a sharp turn that I had to slow down
for. The trailing vehicle gently nudged the back of the
Duster, backed off a few feet, then rammed against my
bumper again. Not cool.

If this was what the local kids did for excitement, I
wanted no more of it. I wasn't terrified; I had been menaced by cars before. But I knew I was in particular danger
due to my unfamiliarity with the road. And in the past
when I had been in the process of being run off the road,
I was in a high-performance vehicle that could shake anything, not a dilapidated old dog like the Duster. It did

appear now that the pickup truck meant business. A couple of nudges on the next two corners were hairy—keeping the Duster on the road in the tight turns was becoming a struggle. The second hit sounded as if it took out a taillight. I decided to slow down well below the speed limit and hope the driver would tire of this game and go find someone else to play with. I slowed to twenty-five miles per hour, assuming the truck would shoot past me at the next opportunity, and the occupants would flip me the bird and disappear into the night. Instead, the truck peeled off to the right, down what looked like a private dirt road. I could see dust fly in the lights before they vanished behind a thickly wooded lot.

Loosening my grip on the wheel, I took a deep breath and felt my heart rate ease back to normal. So I almost certainly had been watched while I was aboard the *Eva B.* As for what had just happened—it felt more like a warning than a full-fledged attack. Maybe I was close to uncovering something after all. Maybe when the *Spartacus* had attacked the boat I was on with Dane and Quasar, the assault had been intended for me and had nothing to do with aquaculture. And if so, the occupants of the truck were aware that I was armed and willing to do more than just bear that constitutional right.

Reminding myself that the dirt road the truck had taken could loop back onto the road on which I drove, I couldn't let my guard down yet. For the next few miles, I drove slowly, taking time to peer down all roads to my right, looking for headlights. I realized that the driver of the truck had been smart enough not to allow me to see a license plate. I wasn't completely comfortable until I reached the causeway that led directly into Green Haven. The man-made causeway was a series of S curves lined on either side by granite blocks I supposed were meant to keep cars on the road and out of the water that lapped the edges at high tide. I relaxed when I hit the south end of the causeway, knowing that I had only three miles to go before I'd be pulling into the lot outside my apartment. I imagined the Vickersons were enjoying their first cocktails by now and would invite me to join them. I wondered what mussel dish they had concocted for tonight's dinner and knew that whatever it was, I would eat it. My stomach growled.

A large shadow appeared in the fringe of my headlights' beam. The shadow moved into the middle of the road and became something quite substantial. I slammed on the brakes and jerked the steering wheel to the right, managing to avoid contact with the deer that jumped in a single, effortless bound back into the woods. The Duster came to a full stop perpendicular to the road and straddled both lanes. The headlights lit up the stand of straggly spruce trees into which I had seen the white underside of the doe's tail vanish. The clump of trees was surrounded by what looked like thoroughly cleared land. I waited and watched for the deer to spring out into the opening on either side of the trees. When nothing moved, I thought of the "deer in the headlights" phenomenon. It was a rather tiny patch of woods. Why couldn't I see the deer's eyes shining brightly in the Duster's lights? I pulled off the road and onto a narrow gravel shoulder, keeping my attention on the trees for motion. How could an animal of that size vanish with one leap? The doe had certainly not vanished. The deer must be close, but I just couldn't see her. As nervous as I was about being pursued, and now riled up by the near miss with a deer, I decided to take a few seconds to get my wits about me before getting back on the road.

The doe's heart must be pounding as hard as mine. After all, she was the one who could have been killed. This brought to mind Parker Alley. Fear is the best motivation for successful and creative disappearing acts, I thought—fear and greed. The same goes for murder— fear and greed are in the top three motives. Was Parker Alley dead, or had he simply disappeared? Had I been as close to him as I now was to the deer and simply not seen him? Until he surfaced, dead or alive, there would be much speculation and intrigue in Cobble Harbor. His disappearance would never get the attention that came when Amelia Earhart or Jimmy Hoffa went missing, of course. Parker Alley was just a fisherman. He would never have a cultlike following like D. B. Cooper, who disappeared in 1971 after hijacking an airplane, collecting $200,000 ransom, and parachuting into the Washington State wilderness, never to be seen again. And yet, if folks here started to think of him as more missing than dead, it would certainly be the cause of a lot of chatter.

The short minute to stop and think had done the trick. My nerve endings had stopped jingling and I was breathing normally. Realizing that I was probably putting myself in danger by spending time parked at the

side of the road looking for that one lucky deer, I decided
to hightail it back to town.

I soon found myself within Green Haven proper,
where the occasional streetlamp illuminated dimly and
fleetingly the interior of my car. Back in my own neighborhood, I allowed my mind to wander a bit as I drove
up the hill toward home. A string of unsolved missing-
persons cases that I had worked on in Florida had simi-
larities to my new case. All of the people in question had
been alone at sea—four cases in a row of people gone
missing while sailing single-handedly. Their boats had
all been found abandoned. The first was deemed an accidental falling overboard, the second was considered
suicide, the third a copycat, and the fourth . . . well by
the time the fourth boat was found unmanned, the investigation of the first had turned up some dirt on the
missing sailor. Digging deeper, my investigative team
learned that all four had reasons to disappear. Bank accounts, investments, properties—everything had been
liquidated shortly after the people went missing and before anyone got suspicious. We believed that all of them
had staged their own deaths until body number two was
found and it was clear that the man had been tortured.
When a second body floated in in the same condition,
we knew we had a serial situation to deal with. Televised
news of the second corpse and a leaky police department
put an end to the killings at sea for a while. Months later,
three boats were found in four days off North Carolina.
The next, three months after that, were off Delaware,
bringing the count to ten. No more bodies were found,

but assets disappeared quicker than officials could secure them. The absence of corpses in the more recent
cases was an indication, to those involved in seeking
justice, that the perpetrators had perfected the art of
body disposal. Maybe the murderous party had moved
up the coast to fresh ground, I thought as I climbed the
stairs to my apartment. It had been three months since
the last strike.

I flipped on all the lights. Just then, it dawned on me
that I was stretching too far. I must certainly be over-
tired, and lack of nutrition had probably resulted in
blood sugar low enough to cause my mind to run ridiculously amok. There was no reason for me to believe that
there was any connection between the disappearance of
Parker Alley and the other ten cases that were never
solved. That's the cop in me, I thought, always trying to
close a case—even at the expense of the facts. There was
no chance of pounding this square peg into that round
hole, even with a bigger hammer. Parker Alley was not in
the same financial strata as the others who had gone
missing off boats. All ten of them had been indepen-
dently wealthy and sailing expensive vessels, not lobster
boats or anything like them. Born into wealth, none of
the ten had ever worked a single day. None of them had
ever gotten married or had children. That may have in-
fluenced the amount of energy we put into our investigations, something I'm loath to admit. When there's no
pressure from a family, it's easier to drop the ball. Someone had done their homework on the victims, that's for
sure.

It was then that I noticed a note had been left on my sofa.

Dear Jane,
I have taken the Mrs. on an epicurean expedition to Nova Scotia. We hear the mussels are fabulous there— and much less expensive than the local. We expect to be back by Friday with samples unless we get waylaid. So until then, I guess you're on your own kiddo!

                                                        Mr. V

My first thought was, Hooray! My second thought was, Who will feed me? And my final thought was, When have the Vickersons ever paid for mussels? Ravenous to the point of nausea, I had to eat right away. I practically ran down the stairs, through the gift shop, and out to the parking area. With the luck I'd had in the Duster so far today—between the game of chicken and the near collision with a full-grown Bambi—I thought it would be wise to walk to the café and see what Audrey had on special. I hustled right along, my pace quickened by hunger and anticipation of being entertained by Audrey's antics. Five minutes later I was bursting through the door of the fully lit and totally empty restaurant. The clang of the cowbells swinging on the door brought Audrey from the kitchen to greet me, her only customer. She hadn't spiked her hair up today, and aside from the glitter on her cheeks and her gigantic yin and yang earrings, she looked sort of normal.

"Hi, Jane! Come in and have a seat. Where've you been? We missed you this morning. The Old Maids and

I debated the cultural importance of rap music." Audrey rolled her eyes and smiled as she pointed to a seat at the counter, where I assumed she wanted me to sit. Before I could answer her question as to my recent whereabouts, she put her hands on her hips and gave me a serious once-over. Shaking her head, she said, "If you ever want your status to change, you really need to be more careful about how you come out in public."

"Status?" I asked. I looked down at the clothes I had worn for the last two days. They had been soaked wet and then slept in and looked it. I wondered how bad my hair was.

"Yup, status. You know, single and available, bordering on desperate."

"I'm too hungry to refute the desperate part," I said with a grin and then quickly pulled my lips down over my teeth before Audrey commented on my oral hygiene. "What's the special?"

"Well, if you came in here more often at night instead of mooching off your landlords, you'd know that Wednesday is Chinese night. That's why we have no customers—it's awful."

"Well, that explains the earrings. I thought Wednesday was Prince Spaghetti day."

"Italian night is Friday, not Wednesday. Don't ask. This is the chef's way of going out on a culinary limb, being bold enough to serve fried rice on the traditional pasta day." Audrey slapped a sheet of paper on the counter in front of me; it was the menu. "You like my earrings? Taijitu—commoners say yin and yang. These symbolize the foundation of the entire universe. Harmony in nature, balance in life; it's all about the unity of opposites. Would you like to borrow them? Anytime but Wednesday."

"If you think they'd help improve my status," I said as I read the menu. "I'm starving. I'll start with an appetizer. What would you recommend—the egg roll or the soup?"

"That's asking me to choose the lesser of two evils. They're equally bad."

"I'll take one of each."

"Perfect." Audrey whisked the menu from my hand and disappeared through the swinging doors to the kitchen.

"I'll take an order of fried rice, too," I yelled after her. Her response was muffled, but the tone was somewhere in between a condolence and a "You'll be sorry." It was indeed unusual to be the only patron. I was glad to learn that Audrey was her usual wisecracking self—even when she had an audience of just one. Usually, she had the Old Maids and Clyde Leeman as her targets, and a large and appreciative crowd. I was happy to have my own turn to be the butt of her jokes and teasing. Though only nineteen, Audrey is precociously self-assured and comfortable in her own tattooed and pierced skin. Most people her age who go to such lengths to alter themselves physically are either hiding something or simply trying to fit in with their peers. But our Audrey was the real deal—fully authentic. From the moment I met her, I felt that Audrey was destined for greatness. I, like everyone else in town, wanted her to like me, and was glad that she did.

With appetizers in hand, and representation of the entire universe dangling from her earlobes, Audrey pushed back through the saloon-style doors. "So, Marilyn comes in this morning with an iPod dangling from her hairy ears. I almost threw up. Seeing someone that old listening to music with anything more modern than a box with a hand crank is disgusting. It's like realizing that your parents had sex," she said as she set the food at my place setting.

That must have been what led to the rap discussion. I stirred the cup of soup with my teaspoon. The liquid was gray, and there were no chunks of anything in it. I slurped a spoonful. "This tastes like dishwater," I said, pushing the cup away and pulling the egg roll closer.

"Great! Is it hot enough?"

"Just right."

"That's what we like to hear. Your fried rice is up. Can I get you some mustard for the egg roll?"

Assuming her next question would be whether I preferred French's or Grey Poupon, I shook my head and nibbled the edge of the egg roll, testing before inhaling. The egg roll wasn't half bad. I ate it in three bites and looked forward to the rice. When the plate of what was advertised as fried rice was set in front of me, I couldn't help looking at Audrey with a questioning raised eyebrow. She cocked her head to one side and forced the cheesiest grin I had ever seen. "Bon appétit," she whispered and continued to stare as I picked up my fork and gingerly sampled the dish.

"Are you sure you didn't mix my order up with some-one else's? This isn't fried rice."

"Right. It's leftover white rice from last night's chicken special with some soy sauce on it. Waste not, want not," she quoted. "Or in this case, perhaps just the latter." Al-though she didn't let on, I could tell that Audrey was amazed that I was able to eat the rice. It really didn't have any taste at all, but it satisfied my hunger and I was fairly confident that it was the safest main course on the menu that night. "Listen, I can hear Marlena calling their cats," Audrey said, cupping an ear with her hand. "They get a little nervous on Wednesdays, living so close to the Chi-nese kitchen."

Now I laughed. The rice had kept my hunger at bay, and I was ready for pie and coffee. Audrey promptly cleaned and reset my place and served what looked like half an apple pie to me. It was delicious. The only things I could always count on at the café were coffee and pie. As bad as the meal was, it was nice to eat something other than mussels for dinner. Audrey left me to enjoy dessert while she breezed around the room, setting up tables for the breakfast crowd. When she returned, she poured me another cup of coffee and said, "So where have you been? When you left here yesterday, you were headed to Cobble Harbor to make a drug bust. How'd that go?"

So much had transpired in the last thirty-six hours. This was an opportunity to hash all of it over with a good listener and possibly catch something I had missed. I told Audrey everything, leaving out no detail. I described the scene in the parking lot where I met George Paul and told her about *Quest, Spartacus,* and the dead body. She listened politely as I went through my experience in Southwest Harbor and the surprise I had when I learned that the corpse was not Parker Alley. I told her about the truck that rammed me, then disappeared. I even told her about the deer. I went through my mental list of follow-up tasks for the next day, realizing for the first time how ambitious the list was. "Wow" was Audrey's response when I finally looked for one. I admitted that I was pretty anxious about talking to Lillian.

Recalling that Audrey had said that Jason was a friend of hers, I saw an opportunity to ask a few questions that I couldn't put to Lillian, who had made it crystal clear that the topic of her son was strictly off-limits. "Did Jason work for his father in the stern of his boat?"

"Are you kidding? Jason absolutely despised his father. Absolutely despised him."

11

THE COWBELLS JANGLED against the door as two young couples entered the café, stealing my chance to ask Audrey if she knew why Jason hated his father so much. My romantic ideal of the Maine father and son being an inseparable team was shattered like the Duster's taillight. Disenchanted and full of apple pie, I stared absently at the paper placemat while Audrey directed the foursome to a nice table by the window, where she suggested they "keep an eye out for a cat if you have a hankering for anything other than the tofu or the vegetable lo mein." The group laughed. They apparently hadn't eaten here before.

Every business in Green Haven advertised on the toffee-colored placemats here at the café. Even the Old Maids, whose shop across the street had a gas pump outside and carried everything from hardware to panty hose—a true Maine variety store—made sure their store was featured on the mat in the same brown, boxy typography that everyone used, but with a small picture of one of the ladies' prized Scottish Fold cats. The cats had nothing to do with their business, as they certainly didn't breed them or sell them; but you could always count on seeing one or two curled up at the cash register or wandering the aisles. And a cat certainly made for a prettier ad than a picture of a gas pump would have, and might attract some strangers looking for pet supplies, which, mysteriously, the Old Maids didn't stock. Once a customer was in the store, Marilyn and Marlena could sell that person a myriad of useless un-pet-related goods, and shame them into tossing pocket change into a jar to raise funds for some unfortunate local or to support Green Haven's Little Leaguers. A coffee stain circled the space marked YOUR AD HERE, leading me to believe there was room for another business in town. Maybe I should start my own private-investigating service. I had always wanted to be self-employed, but could never quite reconcile myself to giving up a sure thing, like a paycheck twice a month. Besides, I didn't imagine there was much need for a private eye in a place where people sweep things under rugs and forget about them. I had read every ad twice by the time Audrey had served Cokes to the two couples and taken their food orders. Finally, she returned to refill my mug with a little more coffee.

I placed my hand over the cup and thanked her before she poured. I explained that I was sure the next couple of days would be hectic, and I needed to go home and get a good night's sleep, something that would be impossible if I caffeinated myself any more. She cheerfully whipped my check from the pocket in her apron and slapped it on the counter with a flourish that, as always, exemplified her abundance of energy and highlighted my lack of it. She disappeared into the kitchen, saying that she hoped to see me back for coffee in the morning before I could question the high price of the soup that I couldn't drink and whether I should actually have to pay for it at all. Oh well, she had been generous with the pie. I plunked a salt shaker on my last ten-dollar bill, exited the café, and headed home.

Exhaustion caught up with me before I crested the first hill, but I forced myself to pick up the pace and made it home in short order. Dragging myself up the stairs, I knew I had only one thing to do before hopping into bed. I needed to call Cal and line up a boat ride to Cobble Harbor for tomorrow morning. After scolding me for calling so late—eight o'clock—his wife, Betty, put Cal on the phone. A short chat included Cal's teasing me about my gourmet dinner and assuring me that Chinese night at the café was indeed a prime example of getting what you pay for. Cal then accepted my offer of work tomorrow, as I knew he would, and agreed to meet at seven thirty for a quick coffee before boarding the *Sea Pigeon*. I hung up the house phone and glanced at my cell. I was surprised to see that someone had left a message, and then delighted to hear Dane Stevens's voice on my voice mail reporting that he had gotten my message and that he and Quasar would certainly pay close attention, and notify me first if they noticed anything out of the ordinary. He thanked me for rescuing his sleeping bag from the corpse, and said that he was sure we'd see each other soon. That was hopeful, I thought.

Sleep came easily. I woke as the first light climbed in orange streaks over the hills on the eastern horizon and settled, filling in the valleys like a syrupy juice before

thinning and allowing blue sky to appear. I was refreshed
and excited about the day ahead. And what a beauty it
was! My mood indicated that my batteries had been
properly charged. The benefits of a good night's sleep are
relatively unsung in today's world of spas, energy drinks,
and herbal supplements. And the best thing about sleep:
It's free.

I wasn't surprised to find Cal already seated and sipping a cup of tea when I arrived at the café fifteen minutes
before our scheduled meeting time. I took the stool beside him that he had clearly saved for me; every other seat
was occupied and a few people hung inside the door
waiting. A cup of coffee appeared from nowhere accompanied by a ghostly voice that made some smart crack
about status and desperation. "Want to split a bagel?" I
asked Cal. "I can expense it."

"Let's go Dutch treat," Cal offered, as a plate piled
high with eggs, sausage, fried potatoes, and toast was
set in front of him. "You'll probably want the second
half of that bread doughnut for your lunch."

"Is that the special?" I asked Audrey as I pointed to
Cal's feast. I was happy to see that she had retired yin
and yang and had replaced them with multiple studs.

"That's the six ninety-nine."

"Whoa! That's too high for me. What's the special
this morning?" I asked, feeling like I wanted to splurge,
but knowing I'd be riddled with guilt.

"The special is *two* ninety-nine. Want it?" she asked
as she dashed by in the opposite direction.

"But what *is* the special? Eggs? Pancakes?"

A loud voice called from the kitchen that an order was up, hastening Audrey's pace in that direction. She opened her eyes wide in question and hesitated just long enough for me to say, "Yes, please."

"One special" was all I heard from the kitchen as the doors swung closed behind Audrey. It sure smelled good in here this morning. I wasn't a picky eater, and I knew that breakfast was always good at the café. So it was fine that I had no idea what I had ordered. When Audrey reappeared with a bagel and cream cheese, I was pleased, but thought it was a bit expensive. "What kind of juice would you like?" she asked.

"No thanks, Aud. I don't care for any."

"It's included with the special."

"Can I have—"

"No substituting."

"Do you have V8?" I asked.

"Tomato."

"Grapefruit?"

"We're out. Orange?"

"No thanks. I don't feel like orange," I said and tried to decide whether I would like tomato after all.

"What *do* you feel like?" Audrey looked a little irritated now as she really needed to hustle to tend to all of her customers.

"Scrambled eggs," I answered honestly. Audrey seemed fed up with my lack of cooperation. She curled her top lip and scurried away to clear a table that had just been vacated. "What's eating her?" I asked Cal, who only shrugged in reply. I spread the cream cheese on my bagel and munched away, trying to get Audrey's attention each time she passed to ask for the tomato juice I had coming. I'd be damned if I would pay three bucks for just a bagel. I would drink the juice even if I didn't enjoy it. I had just finished the last bite of the first half of the bagel when Audrey presented a tall juice glass filled to the brim with steaming, fluffy, scrambled eggs. "Thanks," I said with a smile that went unnoticed as Audrey turned toward the kitchen with an armload of dirty dishes.

Cal was finishing his second cup of tea and looking at his watch when I heard a familiar voice I couldn't quite place. Wrapping my leftover bagel half in a napkin and sticking it in my bag, I looked around to see from whom the distinct voice had come. "Sounds like the pilot, Willard Kelley," Cal said just as I spotted the hulking figure taking up one side of a booth designed for four diners. Cal was right on. Kelley was louder than he needed to be, as men often are who have spent too much time around diesel engines. I told Cal that I would meet him at the dock in a few minutes as I had a bit of business to attend to with the pilot. Cal left what I thought was a ridiculously large tip, making me feel better about shorting Audrey a few cents to avoid having to ask her to make change for a larger bill. She'd appreciate that, I was sure.

Kelley recognized me as I approached and smiled a friendly hello. He appeared to be fresh out of the shower. His graying hair was parted too close to his ear, requiring some kind of goop to defy the natural tendency of gravity. We made a bit of small talk, through which I learned that Willard Kelley was here meeting with his new pilot boat captain and with the man's stern help. He introduced the men. Kelley had a cruise ship coming in to Bar Harbor and needed a ride out. Just like at our first meeting, I couldn't determine whether Kelley was half drunk or fully hungover. They had to leave soon, he explained. I told him that I was assigned to file a police report for his stolen boat, to which he replied, "No need, dear. I won't beeeeee pressing any charges. The boat's back on her mooring, safe as caaaan be." I went on to explain that *Spartacus* had been involved in a little criminal mischief while reported stolen and asked if he had any ideas about who had borrowed her, to which he replied, "I can guarantee you it was the Indian chief."

"George Paul?" I asked.

"That would beeee the one. That guy has quite an enormous sense of entitlement! He helps himself toooooo anything and everything. It has something to doooo with their ideas of ownership. The lazy bastards don't haaaaave anything because they don't work. And they resent anyone who does."

I thanked Kelley for his time and asked how I might get in touch to follow up. He explained that since his new captain lived in Green Haven, he'd be in town quite often on his way to or from a ship. He liked the café and figured this would become his new haunt. I thought this was unlikely. As soon as Audrey became irritated with his volume and weird way of speaking, not to mention his enlightened opinions, she would run him out. I had now decided that Willard Kelley didn't just make a bad first impression; the more you got to know him, the tougher

he was to like. So I would not give him any friendly advice regarding how to handle—or, rather, stay out of the
way of—Audrey. Secretly hoping that she would find
some reason to lash into him this very morning, I hurried
out and down to the dock where Cal had the *Sea Pigeon*
warming up. He had already let the bow and spring lines
go. The pretty little boat leaned lightly against her stern
line, like a dog into a collar when bored with heeling.

I pointed at the stern line. Cal nodded, indicating
that, yes, he was ready for me to cast us adrift. I stepped
aboard, holding the line that I had removed from a cleat
on the dock, and we were off. Just about every mooring in
the commercial harbor was held by a skiff or rowboat,
which meant that the fishermen of Green Haven were out
in force today, anxious to benefit from prices that were
finally rising after the high-season glut. The mood of the
entire town fluctuated along with the market price and
supply of lobster. Virtually every person in Green
Haven—even people far removed from fishing—was in
tune with the industry. Amazing, the degree to which the
ugly little crustaceans referred to by the locals as "bugs"
rule Down East Maine. The Old Maids could quote market price on any given day and recite statistics of flux and
stasis in landings going back a decade.

As we exited the channel and entered the bay, Cal
pushed up the throttle to a comfortable steam. The *Sea
Pigeon* seemed to lift the hem of her skirt out of the spray
created by the increased speed. She skipped lightly between blue puddles that reflected every ray of sun. "This

is a great boat, Cal," I said in admiration for the *Sea Pigeon*'s grace. Cal smiled in thanks; I had given him one of the greatest compliments you can give to someone who has dedicated himself to the sea. I had never spoken to Cal about his life. But I knew that he had won the respect of everyone in town for his accomplishments offshore. Cal was, I thought, the epitome of the able-bodied seaman, even now in his seventies. And he handled the *Sea Pigeon* with a touch as light as that of a man on his wife's back while leading her through a waltz to their song. He reminded me of my poor pal Archie, stuck in that damn Florida prison. Cal lit a cigarette, and I wished he didn't smoke.

We were soon slowing to an idle and rounding the first channel marker leading to Cobble Harbor. The *Sea Pigeon* settled deeply, pulling the surface up like a blanket. Swinging around and through alternating red nuns and green cans, we left the thoroughfare and headed for the town dock. Like Green Haven's, Cobble Harbor's commercial fleet was enjoying this calm day offshore. As late fall approached, it would bring great wind, and fair days like this would become scarce. Cal weaved a crooked path to the dock through a mooring field littered with rowboats. A gentle landing allowed me to reach a piling with the stern line, and I quickly looped it with a clove hitch. Cal wrapped a midship line around a piling and then back to the cleat from whence it came. He then made it fast with a jerk and called it good. He killed the engine and looked quite deliberately at his wristwatch.

"I have no idea how long I'll be, Cal. But I assume it'll be afternoon before you see me back here." I climbed from the boat to the dock.

"Take your time. I ain't going nowhere," he said in his usual pleasant way. "Except maybe to poke around town a bit for lunch. I won't worry about you, but when should I start worrying? Where will you be?"

I thought it was sweet that Cal would be concerned and decided that I would meet him back here at three o'clock to touch base. I explained that I should be ready to head home by then, but if I hadn't quite finished with Lillian, I would at least let him know at that point how much longer I'd be. He agreed with the plan and asked for Lillian's address just in case. I didn't have an address, but gave Cal the same directions to find her house that she had given me. Cal was the perfect partner, I thought, as I approached the parking area between the docks and Main Street. Unlike some of the partners I had been assigned through the years who were anxious to stab me in my back as opposed to covering it, Cal had no desire whatsoever to take over my job. But then again, who would want my current job? Deputy sheriff was not exactly a coveted position, and the insurance gig had gone unfilled and unapplied for until I decided to see if they wanted me to try it. Neither position had prestige or power. There wasn't even much pay.

The parking lot was full to capacity—mostly pickup trucks with bumper stickers promoting local seafood or ridiculing tourism or the federal government. As I turned onto Main Street, I heard an engine start behind me. I made my way to the sidewalk just as the truck turned onto the street headed in the opposite direction, nearly on my heels. The proximity of the vehicle made me turn around to look. I wasn't sure, but it certainly could have been the same truck that George Paul had jumped into the other day. But it could just as easily not have been the same truck. So what was the point of noticing the truck? I wondered. I guess it had struck me as strange that a truck would suddenly leave a full parking lot when I hadn't seen anyone around or any movement since we came into the dock. It occurred to me that I was slipping into my usual habit of overthinking things. What if Willard Kelley had been correct about George Paul stealing his boat? And maybe I had been the target, rather than aquaculture, after all. But what on earth would George Paul have against me? Ridiculous, I realized. It just *seemed* like someone had been hanging out in the parking lot until we had arrived. Real spies were far more discreet. Even local Maine ones.

I turned left onto Quarry Road and walked the half mile Lillian had guessed was the approximate distance to Cobble Harbor's public square. Park benches made with slabs of speckled granite looked as though they had sunk into plush, green moss. A right turn when I was across from the fishermen's monument and a left up a long hill brought me to the end of a narrow road. The gate, although clearly marked PRIVATE, was wide open. I entered as Lillian had said I should, and walked around a sharp bend in the road that opened up to a stately home in a clearing. Funny, I would have assumed this was a summer house belonging to a wealthy Bostonian or New York, not the home of the missing fisherman.

Lillian stood waiting behind a screen door in the center of a room with many large windows. The screen occluded, but couldn't conceal, the sadness in her face. She opened and held the door for me as I entered. Antiques and art melded and gave the house a refined feel. Elegant, yet homey—a combination not usually pulled off so tastefully. My eye was caught by wondrous sea creatures, sculpted from stone. I would have to ask her who had created them. Lillian ran a hand the length of a marble seal that almost seemed to preen with the attention. I complimented the piece. "Edgar Holmes—all of them. This was our first purchase, and we made it before he was discovered. The beauty is simple and innocent. I think that's why I can't walk by without touching this one," she said. "I named him Oscar," she added as she held the seal's chin in her palm. It did seem like she had to make a real effort to pull her hand away, and I guessed that was due largely to what the rest of the day promised. She can't have been looking forward to our conversation.

I followed Lillian through a long hallway dotted with seascapes in oil. "I think I have everything you asked to see," she said as we entered the kitchen. "And I've requested updated statements from banks, credit cards, and the phone company, which they have all promised to e-mail today." Stacks of file folders covered most of the square kitchen table, and a laptop computer sat on a linen placemat at a seat I assumed was hers. A cordless phone lay on an open notebook next to a ceramic shell that held pens and pencils. "Shall I put on a pot of coffee?" she asked.

"Thanks, that would be nice." I pulled one of the eight Windsor chairs from the table and took a seat by a window that overlooked Cobscook Bay. "Your place is lovely. I hope you don't mind my saying that it's so much more than I expected. I guess I have a mental image—stereotype—of a fisherman's house. And it's just not like this at all."

"Modest was not what Parker wanted. He's an extremely hard worker and a very shrewd businessman. You'll see when you get into that stack that he made some good investments and has more than lobster traps providing for us." She opened a door exposing a large, full pantry. "That's not to take away from his ability to catch fish. He's good at what he does and always went the extra mile to make the most of it. He even ships his catch himself to avoid the middleman." I was aware that Lillian was waffling between present and past tense when talking about her husband. She found an electric coffee grinder and a glass French press and placed them on the counter between us. Real coffee, I thought excitedly. I hadn't had a decent cup since I left Miami, a city where connoisseurs raved about their favorite blends and where I fell in love with plain old delicious Dunkin' Donuts java. I hadn't found gourmet coffee in Green Haven, and wouldn't pay for it if I did, and the nearest Dunkin' Donuts is miles away.

Lillian swung open the freezer side of the most spacious side-by-side unit I could imagine. The freezer was jam-packed from top to bottom with zippered one-gallon plastic bags, each one appearing to be crammed full of coffee beans. She grabbed a bag, almost causing a land-slide, and then closed the door. "Wow," I said. "Do you have trouble sleeping? I don't think I have ever seen that much coffee."

Her green eyes hinted at a sparkle. "Isn't it ridicu-lous?" she asked. She opened the door of the freezer again, looked in at all the bags, and then shook her head with a laugh. "There's no room for anything else! Parker is always being given bags of coffee beans as gifts from the ships he delivers the pilot to. When he first started hiring himself out as the person who would deliver the pilot to the ships to guide them into the harbor and then pick the pilot up once they were safely at sea again, the ships were always giving him bottles of liquor in appre-ciation for his service. He said it was one of the perks. Only thing was, we don't drink. He finally told them that we couldn't give away any more booze, so they began with the coffee beans. We have beans from all over South and Central America. We've given tons away as gifts, and still have more than we'll ever use." Her explanation made me recall the scotch whiskey Willard Kelley had in his bag when Cal and I picked him up from the *Asprella*. "These are my favorite beans; they're from Guatemala." Lillian held up what must have been five pounds of very black, oily-looking beans. "Would you like to take some home when you go?"

"I would love to. Thanks," I said. This was a treat that I could share with my landlords when they got home

from their mussel-scouting trip. I quickly got down to the
business of tackling the file folders to get a sense of Parker
Alley on paper. I really wanted to question Lillian, but
didn't think I should start in quite yet. Everything was
fairly well organized. Statements were in chronological
order with the most recent on top. Lillian kept me company as I read. We both sipped coffee until the pot was
empty. I couldn't find anything unusual—except for the
large amount of money they had. The fishermen I had
known who owned and operated their own small boats
barely survived. Parker Alley was indeed a smart inves-
tor. Archie had always told me that a hardworking fisherman who didn't blow his money on the usual bad habits
and addictions could do very well. But until now, I had
never really seen an example of that. I found where Parker's life insurance policy had been upped from $100,000
to $200,000—certainly the timing could be seen as a red
flag, I thought. But the amount did nothing to arouse
suspicion in light of the value of the entire portfolio. I
continued to pore through the pages well past the time
that my stomach suggested lunch. "Have you had a
chance to put together a list of your husband's enemies,
or been able to figure out if anyone might have wanted to
do him harm?" I asked when I couldn't stand waiting any
longer.

Lillian tucked a loose tendril of auburn hair back into
the knot on the back of her head from which it had escaped. She concentrated on swishing around in the bottom of her START YOUR DAY WITH THE LORD mug what
would be a last sip of coffee. Although she appeared to be

thinking, I suspected she was avoiding thought. She began to weep. I waited patiently for a response. Her hands
began to shake and she sobbed. She had seemed so strong
yesterday. Maybe it was just too soon. Eventually, she
wiped the tears from her cheeks and eyes, swallowed,
and took a deep breath. Good, I thought, she was pulling
herself together. "I want to find your husband. I just need
something, anything. A list of his enemies would be very
helpful."

"Evan is putting that together for you. But the list will
be incomplete," she stated as a matter of fact.

"Really? How so?" I asked.

"Evan won't have included my name—and it belongs
right at the top."

12

ALTHOUGH I WAS CERTAIN that I'd heard Lillian correctly when she said that her own name should be at the top of the list of her husband's enemies, I asked her if she could repeat what she'd just said, hoping that she would do so and tell me more. She did and did. Like most confessions, hers was tearful. Unlike most, this was one I had not anticipated. It seemed that Lillian Alley was convinced that she had driven her husband to take his own life. "We had a terrible fight," she began. "The night before Parker went missing, I called him a coward and said that if he were any kind of man at all, he would kill himself and be done with his miserable life."

"Did you fight often?" I asked. Lillian said that she and Parker never fought. In fact, they never even argued. She was distraught about the death of their son, she let her emotions get wildly out of hand, and she lost control of her senses. A discussion about nothing turned into a bitter argument that ended with her suggestion that Parker remove himself from this world. He had stayed up all night, she said. And she had lain awake, too, into the wee hours. She finally fell asleep at daybreak and didn't awaken until mid-morning. When she got up, Parker was gone; she presumed he was making a pilot run or hauling lobster traps. She never imagined he would actually harm himself.

Lillian was miserable waiting for her husband's daily radio call. It never came. "I figured he was still upset and didn't want to talk to me. I would never have thought that my hateful words would get to him like that. Then I found the note." Lillian stood and reached into her hip pocket, retrieving a slip of paper. She handed it to me to read.

"You know that in addition to being deputy sheriff, I work as a consultant for insurance companies. Let's just say that once I read this note, I would be required to file a report about its existence. And if your insurance company has proof that Parker's death was a suicide, then they don't have to pay one cent of the policy benefits you would be owed if they came to the conclusion that his death was an accident." I held the note in an open palm for her to take back and destroy if she so chose. I'm all for doing my job, but wanted to make sure I wasn't taking advantage of a widow's grief.

"That money means nothing. I want the truth to come out. I want you to find Parker's body. He was a great man and deserves a proper burial. You've seen the accounts— Parker left me very secure financially. I don't need the pittance the insurance company would love to save. My husband was a good man. And he was a great fisherman. He never would have died in an accident and never would have fallen overboard. He killed himself grieving for our son. I'm afraid I pushed him. But what could be more honorable than a man who can't live without his son?"

I unfolded the shipping receipt and read the scrawled note:

Dear Lillian,
You are right. I am a coward. I hope you'll someday
be able to forgive me. Your life will be better without
me. I have always loved you and always will.

                                        Parker

I refolded the note and stuck it in my bag. "Where did you find it?" I asked.

"In his lunch pail. I was feeling so bad about the fight and everything I had said that I got out of bed and wrote him a note apologizing." Lillian's emotions had stabilized. She was calm and clearly wanted to tell her story. She was convinced that she was responsible for her husband's death. That wasn't something she could share with their family. I was clearly the first person with whom she'd been able to share her terrible secret. "I always pack Parker's lunch the night before and put it in the refrigerator out in his workshop. He leaves before daylight. So I put my note in with his lunch knowing that he would get it at ten when he breaks for a sandwich. He didn't take his lunch pail, but he took my note and left his for me."

"May I see the workshop?" I asked. Of course Lillian was very cooperative, as she now was feeling like a heavy weight had been lifted from her shoulders. I explained to her that, legally, she was not guilty of anything, and re-minded her that people fight and say things they don't mean. I certainly wasn't trying to clear her conscience, but until I was able to uncover the truth, I needed Lillian to be frank with me about everything. And becoming her friend would facilitate that end more than acting like a hard-nosed cop would. If she trusted me, maybe I could get her to open up about her son.

"But I told Parker that I *hated* him. That had to kill him. It would me." I followed Lillian through a back door of the kitchen into a large shop. "Parker spent most of his time at home out here." She flipped on some fluorescent lights. "He was a workaholic. He loved his work more than life itself."

I wandered the floor of the shop and was impressed with the array of tools and the workstations he had organized. At the far end of the room was an air compressor and some type of mechanical contraption that I didn't recognize. Everything surrounding this station was covered with a thick layer of dust. "It doesn't look as though he had used this equipment lately," I said, mostly to myself and not expecting an answer.

"No, you're right. This is where Parker built his lobster traps. Like most young fishing families, we started out with nothing but an old wooden boat and a few rickety traps. Parker had to build his own gear to save money. He took great pride in doing everything possible to cut out the middleman and maximize our income. Look"—Lillian pointed to a workbench to my left—"he even made his own freezer packs for shipping his lobsters and scallops. At first, doing everything himself was a necessity. We were really just scraping by."

"What else, other than fishing, was Parker involved in?" I was still finding it hard to believe that hauling lobster traps—even if you've cut out the middleman—could provide for a family in this style.

"Just work. That's it. No hobbies or anything, if that's what you mean. He fished and saved money, bought a better boat and then a better boat, the same as everyone else around here. A few years ago, Parker had the opportunity to work as the pilot boat, which really helped us out financially. He was the only boat servicing Cobs Bay Pilots, so he had a couple runs a week. Every time a tanker needed to go up the river to the refinery or a cruise ship had a scheduled stop in Bar Harbor, Parker was moonlighting. We were doing fine without the pilot work, but that extra money was all invested and has done well." She stopped long enough to think for a few seconds then added, "The only other thing Parker had going on was that he participated as a volunteer in the U.S. Coast Guard Auxiliary."

"What did that consist of?"

"First of all, Parker never volunteered for anything. He was too busy making money. Some government program provides fuel money for people with boats who agree to patrol and report anything suspicious. No one spends more time on the water than Parker did, so it seemed like a good fit for him to be keeping an eye out, and he was reimbursed for the fuel he would be burning fishing or piloting anyway."

"Did he ever report or mention any suspicious activity to you?"

"No, in fact everyone involved knows it's sort of a way of getting money for nothing from the government. Apparently any seacoast town where there is no military base has been determined by the experts to be at greater risk for terrorist activity. Cobble Harbor? Terrorist attack? It's laughable." Lillian leaned over a chest freezer and opened it, exposing more coffee beans and a small basket filled with freezer packs for shipping. "Having said that, I have to admit that my first thought when I saw the dead man yesterday was that he must be a terrorist and that Parker had killed him. For a brief moment, I thought my husband would be revered as a hero." Lillian hesitated and looked as though her next breath caught in her chest. Her eyes welled up again, but she fought the tears and held them back. "Then I came to my senses and realized that I was still unable to face the fact that Parker had killed himself and that I may have had a lot to do with it. What would terrorists target in Cobble Harbor—the sardine cannery? And with all of the fishermen on the water, someone would have seen a boat that didn't belong."

I was aware of the different incentives offered in the name of Homeland Security, and agreed that Cobble Harbor was the least likely target for terrorism that I could imagine. I walked the perimeter of the shop once more. Parker Alley's shop was in the same condition that his boat had been—superorganized, every tool in a special place, even a custom-built rack to hold delicate scales for weighing. If everything Lillian had said was truthful and accurate, it was quite probable that Parker had committed suicide. And I did have the note he'd written. That didn't explain the corpse, though, with the bait iron in its chest. Maybe there was no connection. It would certainly be helpful to hear from Dane and Quasar that they were headed into Southwest with another body for the family to ID, I thought. Now who was grasping at straws?

After I checked out Parker's inventory of shipping supplies, which were exactly the same kind of supplies I had seen aboard the *Eva B.*, Lillian and I left the shop, returning to her kitchen table without a word. There wasn't much more I could do here without a list of enemies to question and without the promised e-mails from the banks and credit card companies, which I thought I should peruse to see if there was any deviation from the norm. I wanted to begin learning about her son, Jason, and the circumstances surrounding his overdose, but even though Lillian had calmed considerably, I couldn't take her there yet. She had said the account information had been promised by the end of the business day, which probably meant five P.M. on the dot. But I needed to head back to the *Sea Pigeon* soon; if I didn't, I ran the risk of worrying Cal needlessly. "From what you've told me, I don't think your husband would consider you enemy number one," I said. "In fact, I would guess the opposite to be true."

"I think when you mentioned the list, it was an opening for me to blurt all that out before I lost my nerve," Lillian said. That was exactly how I read it. "Evan is putting a list together and will drop it off on his way home from fishing this evening. I can't imagine anything will come of it. I guess Parker had some enemies, mostly people who are jealous of the fruits of his labor. He was certainly center stage in the opposition to the oyster farm, and he had an ongoing feud with the Passamaquoddy Indians over fishing grounds and rights, but those things have never escalated beyond slashed tires or spray paint."

The clock on her microwave oven indicated that it was now 2:40, so I explained that I would be leaving as I needed to catch a ride from the dock at three. I printed my phone numbers—home and cell—on the back of an envelope and asked that she please call me when the information came in and to then also read me the list of names her brother-in-law came up with. She agreed to do so and thanked me for spending so much time with her. "I hope you'll find Parker soon. I need to get on with my life somehow. Right now, I don't know where to begin. For the past seventeen years I've been Parker's wife and Jason's mother. Now I am neither." Although she had mentioned her son's name, I would wait for our next meeting to bring him up myself.

Lillian walked me through the house and held the screen door open for me. Armed with coffee beans and a suicide note, I walked with a brisk pace, hoping to arrive at the *Sea Pigeon* before Cal had even a second of concern. I dug into the bottom of my tote bag and found my cell phone. I turned it on and stared at the signal strength bars as I walked. Three bars, but no messages—par for the course, I thought. I dialed my home number and entered the two-digit code to play messages that might have been left on my machine in the apartment. "You have one new message," the machine squawked. I waited for the message to play and crossed my fingers in prayer to hear Dane Stevens.

"Hello, Deputy Bunker. This is Sheila from the Knox County Sheriff's Department. The Office of the Chief Medical Examiner called and asked us to notify you that fingerprints have confirmed a positive ID on case number two-two-seven-four-fiver. We have a name and passport number. Please call at your earliest convenience. Thank you." Sheila left a number, which I scratched onto the sidewalk with a piece of gravel. This was so exciting, I thought. Finally a breakthrough; I wasn't expecting any word on John Doe this soon. What were the chances of having fingerprints on file? As I dialed the number for the sheriff's office, a truck pulled up beside me and came to a stop. I pushed the red button on my phone, severing the connection but storing the number for when I had privacy.

George Paul leaned across the front seat and rolled down the passenger-side window. "Can I give you a lift?" I had a feeling that this was the truck I had seen leaving the parking lot earlier. Physically, George Paul appeared to have the ability to crush cars with his bare hands, but he carried himself with a rare kind of gentleness. I wanted to ask him where he went after our discussion at the pier the day *Spartacus* attempted to drive *Quest* onto the rocks of the breakwater, but was more anxious to make the phone call to learn the ID of the corpse.

"No thank you. I'm only going to the town dock."

"I'm heading right there. Come on, get in." He opened the door and waited. I hesitated. "Your friend is expecting you back aboard by three, and it's"—he checked his wristwatch—"five minutes to." Although my suspicion of George Paul was growing, the fact that he had spoken with Cal made me feel a bit easier about climbing into the truck with him. Dane Stevens thought he was a nutcase, and Willard Kelley claimed that he was a thief. Two reasons not to accept the ride, I thought as I pulled myself up and in and slammed the door. I left the window open and rested an elbow in the door frame. George Paul drove slowly, his hands dwarfing the steering wheel.

"Nice truck," I said.

"Thanks. It's not mine. I'm borrowing it." I wondered if I was riding in a stolen vehicle. Since I wasn't in town to investigate that, I really didn't care. "How was your boat ride the other day?" he asked. That could have been interpreted as a signal for me to get the hell out of the truck. If he knew that we were menaced on the water, then it was a question with a sinister edge. If he didn't know, then it was just a question. I decided it was the latter and that George Paul was fishing.

"Fine. How was yours?"

"Fine, thanks. Did you and your friends find what you were hoping to?" he asked.

"Oh, we found something all right. But not exactly what we had hoped for. They're still very confident that the survey will be successful." My mind's eye flashed on an image of the corpse with the faded streak of that red substance, which ran nearly the length of the body. I tensed while again making a connection with George Paul's explanation of the Red Paint People's burial ritual. George Paul held a key to some part of this mystery, I was certain. We arrived in the parking lot, and George pulled into the only empty spot and shut the engine off.

"So the boys must still be looking to make their bonus, right?" he asked as we both opened our doors. I noted that he left the keys dangling in the truck's ignition—just as the drivers had done in nearly every other vehicle in the lot, I assumed, if the folks of Cobble Hill behaved the way people did back in Green Haven.

"There's still time, yes." There was something coy in his manner, and I couldn't figure out what, if anything, he was hiding. When we first met, George Paul had mistaken me for a newspaper journalist and was incredibly talkative. I wondered if he now knew that I was an officer of the law. I certainly wasn't going to volunteer that fact.

I thanked him for the ride and we parted company, taking off by foot in opposite directions. As I walked by the front of the truck, I noticed a smashed headlight and dented grill. This was probably the truck that had harassed me and broken the Duster's taillight. I wondered who George Paul had borrowed it from and who had been behind the wheel of the truck and trying to run me off the road or scare me away from whatever I had gotten too close to. I stopped to enter the license plate number into my cell phone to run later. "It belongs to Parker Alley," George Paul volunteered. I hadn't noticed that he'd stopped and turned back to face me. "I didn't think he'd miss it."

13

NO MATTER WHAT ANYONE told me about George Paul, I couldn't help but like him. He looked like a guy who had spent years sparring with Foreman and Ali; he and I didn't seem to share a lot in common, and I couldn't exactly call him a friend as he was still most accurately described as some guy I'd met in a parking lot. But I just liked him in the same sort of way that I like John Daly—the bad boy of the PGA. I've always been that way—I like who I like. This personality trait first surfaced in middle school when I found myself going steady with Stanley Rodriguez, a kid who basically laid permanent claim to the class dunce cap and who was widely believed to have "cooties." I didn't care. Again, I like who I like.

Happily, the flip side is not part of my makeup. I almost never *dis*like people for no reason at all. When I dislike someone, I have a darn good reason. So did it bother me that I had just sent a small wave of thanks to a man who had yelled across a parking lot for all to hear that he had given me a ride in a truck stolen from a man who was likely on the bottom of the ocean? Not really. George Paul would remain in my mind a good guy until he proved himself otherwise. I was expecting a comment from Cal as I approached the stern of the *Sea Pigeon* and wasn't disappointed. "Didn't your mother warn you about taking rides with strangers?" he asked.

"George Paul isn't a stranger. I met him the other day. Besides, I didn't want to keep you waiting or worry you."

"He's a creep." Another party weighs in, I thought. When I didn't respond, Cal continued. "He was sure concerned about what you were doing at Lillian Alley's house. Of course, I didn't tell him, because I don't know anything. Didn't stop him from asking questions though. Creepy."

So, I thought, George Paul must have followed me to Lillian's. Unwilling to debate "creepy" with Cal, I decided to change the subject. "Let's get out of here. I'm starving. Let the lines go?"

"Sure," Cal said as he loosened a line from the cleat closest to him. I slackened the stern line from a cleat and pulled the bitter end around a piling and back aboard where I coiled and stowed it on a hook under the rail. Cal knocked the boat in gear with the helm hard to starboard, kicking the stern to port and away from the dock. He reversed the engine enough to back the *Sea Pigeon* a distance from the pilings to allow him to pull out while turning to port and to avoid contact with anything solid. Once we were clear of the dock, I grabbed my cell phone from my bag and prayed. Damn! No service. I would have to wait until we made the corner around the steep headland and had a shot at the cell tower on Swan's Island. I tucked the phone back into my bag to avoid staring at it like a teenager waiting for a text message.

Cal tugged a cigarette from a fresh pack in his breast pocket and tucked it into the corner of his lips. He raised an index finger in the air, suggesting I wait for something that had just dawned on him. He grabbed a brown paper bag from the console against the windshield and handed it to me. "There's a nice sandwich shop about a block from the dock," he said. "I figured that doughnut would be wearing thin on you by now. So I got you something. You ain't one of them vegetarians, are you?"

"No. I'm a carnivore." I wasn't surprised that Cal had asked. About all he'd ever seen me eat was peanut butter and bread. Opening the cellophane wrap, I allowed the halves of the sandwich to separate, exposing an inch of pink roast beef. "Wow. Thanks Cal. Want half?" He shook his head and lit his cigarette. He enjoyed his smoke while I indulged in beef. How long had it been, I wondered, since I had eaten roast beef? This must have cost a fortune. I would add a small bonus to Cal's check this week, I thought. Well, that was if it didn't cost too much to repair the Duster's taillight. I could order the lens and bulb from the Old Maids and repair it myself. That would save the labor of a mechanic. The thought of finances tempted me to wrap the second half of the sandwich and save it for dinner. But that might be rude. So I happily ate the whole thing.

Feeling stronger with a belly full of sandwich, I concentrated on organizing my thoughts. I felt that I had collected fragments of the whole picture but was unable to put anything together. If I could just start the puzzle in one corner, I could build from there. It was seldom that I had this much information and still could not formulate a viable theory to tie everything together. Right now I would be satisfied with a solid hunch, even one that might need to be discarded after I had the next clue. But I didn't even have that. I closed my eyes and saw the pieces: Parker Alley, John Doe, George Paul, North Atlantic Shell Farms, Lillian, fishing rights, heroin, and Jason. I shuffled, rearranged, stacked, and played sleight-of-hand games with the pieces. But nothing clicked. Suddenly the *Sea Pigeon* lurched hard to starboard. I grabbed the edge of the console and hung on as we rolled to port and back to starboard in the wake of a passing boat.

When the *Sea Pigeon* settled down, I turned to see the boat behind us. The *Ardency,* Evan Alley's boat, steamed away, throwing a mountainous wake. The captain and stern man never glanced back. "Looks like someone's in a hurry to get to the barn," Cal laughed, happy that I had been jarred from my trance. That made two of us. I added Evan to my puzzle pieces. I remembered how he had been so cool the day his brother's boat was found circling. He had absolutely zero interest in searching for his brother and displayed no hope of finding Parker alive. Yes, Evan deserved some close attention.

I pulled the phone from my tote and held it to the sky in an offering to the god of cellular service. Three signal-strength bars rose from the depths. I hit the button recalling the number for the Sheriff's Department, pushed the green SEND, and walked to the stern, where the engine noise was less bothersome. After two rings, a female voice identified herself as Sheila and asked how she might direct my call.

"Hi, Sheila. This is Deputy Bunker returning your call. I understand you have some information for me regarding a John Doe." I was nervous with anticipation.

"Ah, yes. Let's see. Bunker . . . Oh, here it is. Augusta faxed this and asked me to forward it to you. The man's name is Jorge Aguilar. He was born in November 1970 in Champerico, Guatemala. He was employed by Central American Oil, aboard a tanker that is in and out of U.S. waters. So his fingerprints were on file with Homeland Security."

"Does the report name the tanker?" I asked.

"Well, let's see. I have a passport number. . . . No. Here's a customs form. It's six months old, but at that time he was aboard the *Asprella*. Is that helpful?"

"Yes. Thanks, Sheila. Please let the sheriff know that I'm on this case and will report back with any developments." I thanked Sheila again before we hung up and she seemed genuinely pleased to be of some assistance. I didn't imagine much of her work included dead people from Guatemala.

I joined Cal back at the helm as he eased the throttle to enter the channel that would lead us to the dock in Green Haven. "Cal," I said. "Where was the *Asprella* heading after we picked up Willard Kelley the other day?"

"Halifax, Nova Scotia."

"Is that far from here?" I asked.

"It would be aboard this rig. But I suppose it's like next door for a tanker. They steam at twenty-five knots. Why?"

Why? That was a good question. I answered it in a rather long-winded fashion. I worked backward from the information provided by Sheila. I suppose this was a way for me to think out loud and fill Cal in on everything that I had kept from him until now. I tried to sort things out as I told Cal the details of what I had learned over the last three days, hoping that when I finished, the solution to the puzzle would suddenly be clear. When I got to the part about George Paul's explanation of the Red Paint ritual and the connection I had made to the corpse, Cal laughed. I couldn't imagine what he found funny. "What? It could have been someone framing the Passamaquoddy, right?" I urged Cal to tell me what he thought.

"The red stuff on the dead guy must have been copper paint. You know, that red antifouling paint everyone uses on the bottom of their boats? Originally, you were look-ing for someone you believed had fallen overboard, right?" This was embarrassing, I thought. Of course—it was just paint from the bottom of a boat. Cal continued. "Copper paint—of course, they don't put real copper in it anymore, they just call it that. Still, it makes a wicked red mess on anything that comes into contact with it. I've ruined more clothes coppering the bottom of this boat." The conversation was interrupted; we had just arrived at the dock and needed to concentrate on securing *Sea Pigeon*.

As we walked toward Cal's truck, I mentioned that I had to get in touch with Willard Kelley to learn when the *Asprella* would be in the area again. "Good luck." Cal seemed to be tired and had lost interest in the case. He was happy being the chauffeur. I told Cal that I would let him know in the morning what our next assignment would be. I suspected we would need to return to Cobble Harbor to check on some of the names Evan Alley might come up with, especially those of his brother's enemies. I reminded myself of Cal's age and understood that he was anxious to get home to dinner and an early bedtime. I bid Cal good night, thanking him again for the sandwich. "Kelley's a creep, too" were his parting words. Cal, like most people of his age, gets a little cranky when he's tired, I thought.

We sure had lost a lot of daylight since I had first arrived in Green Haven, I thought, as Cal's brake lights flashed at the stop sign at the junction of the parking lot and Main Street. Anxious to get home to try to locate Willard Kelley and to touch base on the phone with Lillian, I hurried along. By the time I reached the top of the hill, I was gasping for air, and I was totally out of breath when I reached the stairs to my apartment. I had learned the hard way not to call anyone after five P.M. Mainers are strict about dinnertime, and they like to eat early. Most of the people I knew sat down for dinner promptly at five, and anyone foolish enough to interrupt the meal got an earful. I understood that fishermen rise at three A.M. and, in order to get their full eight hours, need to turn in by seven. Even the folks who don't fish keep the same schedule. Except for my land-lords. Henry and Alice prided themselves on their late dinnertime and fancied themselves European. I knew that this was because they liked a two-hour cocktail hour, a double they called it, and didn't feel they could start drinking until five, which pushed supper to the ungodly hour of seven, something basically unheard of in this town.

But the Vickersons were still away, so I was on my own. I pushed open the door, flipped on some lights, and then dropped my bag in a chair and checked the answering machine. No messages. I loosened the buckle on my gun holster, removed it, and hung it on the wooden peg that Mr. V had mounted on the wall among three others for coats. I would secure the gun in its locked case later. Was it just four months ago that I had vowed never to carry a gun again? Well, I had lied. My vows were mean-ingless. I hadn't made a New Year's resolution in ages, because they inevitably brought on deep depression when I breached my contract with myself. I never kept any vow I made unless it was to someone other than me. That was different. And yet I had given Audrey my word the other day that I would put someone in jail. And right now, I seemed to be getting further from that promise. Audrey would never mention it, nor would she rub my nose in the fact that I hadn't been able to deliver. But I'd bet she hadn't forgotten what I had pledged. I certainly wouldn't forget.

I sat at the table with a paper and pen and leafed through the relatively few pages of the local phone book looking for Willard Kelley or Cobscook Bay Pilots. There were a few Kelleys in the "Greater Bar Harbor Region," but no Willard. I struck gold in the Yellow Pages. There was indeed a listing for Cobscook Bay Pilots, Inc., that included two numbers—one for the usual business hours and another for nights and weekends. I quickly dialed the second number, assuming it would forward to Willard Kelley's home phone. A woman, I assumed Willard Kelley's wife, answered.

"Hello, Mrs. Kelley?"

"Yes."

"Hi, Mrs. Kelley. This is Deputy Bunker from the Knox County Sheriff's Department. I'm looking for a Willard Kelley. Is this the correct number?" I asked as politely as I could.

"What will you try next? Give me a break. If you want to whore around with my husband, that's your problem. He's probably dead drunk by now. Stop calling me! Get it?" *Crash!* The phone was slammed down. I removed the receiver from my ear and stared at it in disbelief. Did that really just happen? I had to try again. I dialed the same number and got the same "Hello."

"Hi, Mrs. Kelley. Please don't hang up. This is Jane Bunker. I am a deputy sheriff here in Green Haven and am involved in an investigation, and I urgently need to get the schedule for a tanker your husband pilots."

"Really?"

"Yes, Mrs. Kelley. I'm not looking for your husband. But I do need that schedule. I can come to your home with a warrant if you would prefer."

"No, that's not necessary. Which ship are you look-ing for?" she asked.

"The *Asprella*."

"I'm the secretary here, among other things. I should be able to help you out. What did you say your name was?"

"Jane Bunker. Deputy Sheriff Jane Bunker. I work for the Knox County Sheriff's Department."

"Bunker, okay. Willard had a double today. He took one of the Carnival cruise ships into Bar Harbor this morning and is scheduled to meet the *Asprella* right about now to take her up the river to Bucksport. He'll stay aboard while they pump, then take her back offshore later tonight. She won't be back again until next month. Sorry about hanging up on you."

"That's quite all right. Thanks for your cooperation, Mrs. Kelley." We hung up in a civilized manner this time. Either right now or not until next month! I'd better get a move on. I wondered where I would find the ship once I got to Bucksport, but couldn't take the time to figure that out right now. I had to get going. I strapped my gun back around my midsection, threw on a jacket, grabbed my tote bag, and ran out the door.

I nearly choked when I calculated how much gas I would burn in the four-hour round-trip to Bucksport. If I weren't in such a hurry I could at least ease up on the ac-celerator. But I needed to get there quickly. The sooner I was aboard the ship and asking questions about Jorge Aguilar, the better. Time is not a friend of a murder in-vestigator. Guilty parties can create very elaborate and

convincing alibis given enough time. They can buy witnesses, too. I stepped on the gas pedal even harder. I
knew I would be reimbursed for my expenses. This was
exciting. I tried to contain my nerves as I drove. I pushed
the Duster like I was being chased by something out of a
nightmare. This was exhilarating. Maybe this was a feeling that I'd been missing and hadn't realized it. Pure
adrenaline. Two hours, two hours to Bucksport. I prayed
the *Asprella* would still be in port. Two hours faded to
one hour. I skidded around corners, flew off bumps, and
squealed tires on straightaways. The old Duster was in
top form. How many middle-aged women got to do this?
I was crazed and I loved it.

The light distinguishing Bucksport from the surrounding blackness was a dull haze. Rising from individual bright spots and joining hands, the town's lights
dimmed as they spread upward, forming a cloudy veil
that appeared to protect everything under it. As I entered
the town and got under the umbrella, the haze cleared.
From the middle of a bridge I could see a large terminal
on the west side of the Penobscot River surrounded by
tremendous tanks that looked like overgrown silos. Tugboats were bridling up to the only ship at the terminal.
The bright yellow shell on the ship's stack left no doubt.
It was the *Asprella*. All I had to do was figure out how to
get there, I thought.

I knew I had to turn right. I drove slowly off the bridge
and continued on the main drag until I found a significant right turn—one that looked like it could support
some tractor-trailer traffic. I had guessed correctly. A

chain-link fence hemmed in the tank farm and wharf. A guard shack was manned by an elderly gentleman who tried to tell me I was in the wrong place until I showed him my badge. He waved me through and directed me to park in a spot marked VISITOR. I ran from the parking area to the wharf and sprinted to the section alongside the *Asprella*. A small hydraulic boom was winching up the aluminum gangplank that connected the ship to the top of the dock. I waved to the man running the winch, asking him to stop. "I need to board the ship!" I yelled. He stopped and waited for me to come close enough to talk. "I need to board that ship, right away."

"Do you have an ID, or a visitor's pass?" I whipped out my badge and introduced myself as the Knox County Sheriff, leaving out the deputy part in the interest of brevity. He lowered the gangplank, allowed me to board, and cranked it back up and away.

The deck of the *Asprella* was the size of a football field. Large pipes ran in mazelike confusion to pump boxes and valves that I stepped over as I worked my way toward a set of stairs that went up to the bridge. I needed to find the captain. The ship was made fast to the wharf by steel cables that were now being slacked off of drums to release the ship for departure. The tugboats strained against steel bridles, waiting to take control of the tanker and escort her down the river to the ocean. I banged a couple of hardy knocks on the steel door at the top of the stairs and let myself in. The bridge was massive, and although the overhead lamps had been doused, the electronics—all in duplicate—emitted enough light for me to comfortably see three men. I introduced myself, showing the badge, and asked to see the captain.

A uniformed gentleman shook my hand and asked what I was doing aboard his ship. I explained as briefly as I could that I was investigating the death of Jorge Aguilar and that U.S. Customs records showed that he was employed aboard the *Asprella*. The captain looked pained with the news of the death and quietly introduced the other men as his first and second mates. "Jorge was one of our crew. This is most upsetting. We will, of course, cooperate with your investigation, but right now we're casting off."

"That's okay," I said, relieved that I had indeed found someone who might provide at least one more piece of the puzzle. "I'll hop off at your next stop. I just need a little time to ask some questions of you and Jorge's shipmates."

A voice from the remote radio on the captain's belt said that all lines were clear. The captain took the radio from his hip and handed it to the first mate, who keyed the microphone and said, "Roger." The ship started to move sideways away from the wharf, pulled by the powerful tugs. The captain asked his men to man the helm and radio while the tugs navigated the *Asprella* to the mouth of the river; once there, the ship would be under her own power.

"I have about thirty minutes before I have to pay attention. You, on the other hand, have plenty of time. Our next port is in Central America. Unless you want to jump off with the pilot once we're out of Maine state waters, you can make yourself comfortable in my quarters. I'll move in with the chief engineer."

Central America? I hadn't given this plan much thought, I now realized. "I'll jump with the pilot. It's Willard Kelley, right? Where is he?" The captain explained that "Willy" had had a long day and was freshening up, which I understood to be sobering up. I figured if Willard could get from the ship to the lobster boat in his condition, then I would certainly have no trouble doing the same. "Isn't he supposed to be piloting the ship right now?" I asked. The captain explained that, yes, that was the law. But it seemed that the piloting gig was a formality that cost shipping companies tens of thousands of dollars a year, and totally unnecessary after a captain has been in and out of any given port once. "How long before I bail out?" I asked. The captain explained that I would have ninety minutes before the pilot boat was alongside, and led me to the officers' dining room, where we sat at a small table and were served coffee and pastries by a man who looked a lot like Jorge Aguilar.

Before I revealed the little I knew about the circumstances surrounding Jorge's death, I asked the captain to tell me if and when he had first noticed or been notified that one of his crew members was not around. By the time the captain finished speaking, I had come to regard him as a decent and honest man, which was my first impression anyway. I was pretty certain that he hadn't taken part in, nor had he any knowledge of, wrongdoing aboard his ship. It seemed that the captain had received a call from the home office in Venezuela that Jorge Aguilar's wife was very ill and it was necessary, if Jorge was to see his wife alive, for him to go home to Guatemala right away. The captain excused Jorge from his contract and made arrangements for his travel. The captain bought Jorge a bus ticket from Bangor, Maine, to Boston and plane fare to Guatemala with his own personal credit card; Jorge was to pay him back when he could.

The travel arrangements for Jorge included a ride on the pilot boat. That was the fastest way to get Jorge ashore, since the pilot was on his way to meet the ship to bring her into Machiasport when they got the news about Jorge's wife. The plan had been for the pilot to board the ship, and for Jorge to leave the ship and board the lobster boat to go ashore, where the boat's captain would drive him to the bus station in Bangor. The captain knew that the pilot boat Willard Kelley had been using was the *Eva B.*, and that was the boat that delivered Kelley on that trip. "Did you see Jorge get aboard the *Eva B.*?" I asked.

"Unfortunately not. The shape of the *Asprella*'s hull hides the pilot boat once it gets within striking distance. My job is to maintain course and speed while the lobster boat does the maneuvering alongside and away after transfer. I can't see a thing from the bridge and rely on radio transmissions from the deck. The first I see of Willard is when he climbs over the rail onto the deck and the last I see of him is in the opposite direction."

"That sounds a little hairy."

"It can be, in bad weather. We've never had a mishap, but the minute or so when the pilot is going up or down the ladder out of my sight and the radio is quiet can be fairly long and agonizing."

"Who *can* see the pilot boat and full transfer?" I asked, wondering who to question next. This, I learned, varied from transfer to transfer. The captain said that a couple of crew members always stood at the rail of the ship to assist if needed. In fact, sometimes a man would travel down the ladder to help with the pilot's bag so that the pilot could use both hands while climbing on and off the ladder. One of the crew members was responsible for radio transmissions to the bridge—sort of remote eyes for the captain, he said. So it was immediately clear that I needed to speak with the crew members responsible for the pilot and Jorge's transfer on that leg of their trip three days ago. And I didn't have much time to get what I needed from them. The captain had to resume his responsibilities on the bridge now, so I followed him back up to find Willard Kelley slumped on a bench seat in a corner.

The light that came in through the wheelhouse door from the gangway snapped Willard Kelley to a more attentive posture. He struggled to his feet and greeted me in an overly friendly way. He embraced me with a bear hug that could have crushed my ribs had I not been of hardy stock. He smelled of aftershave and mouthwash, and his hair had been glued into place against a wet-looking forehead. "Jane! How nice to seeeeee you. The mates told me that you were here and why. Such sad neeeeews about Jorge. He was a good man."

I pressed my palms against his chest, forcing him to release his grip on my shoulders. He teetered, but quickly found his sea legs and balanced, holding the edge of a radar screen. "Hello, Mr. Kelley." I tried for a professional tone somewhere between friendly and brusque. "The captain has explained the arrangements he made for Jorge's travel, and what I need from you is a statement as to when you last saw him. My understanding, if I have it right, is that you were boarding the *Asprella* and Jorge Aguilar was disembarking this ship and boarding the *Eva B.* to be taken ashore."

"Yes, yes, that's all correct. Jorge and I were like two ships passing in the night—and it waaaaas at night as I recall. I can check for an exaaaact time in my log. Jorge scrambled down the side of the ship, I handed him my baaaag, which he placed on the hook to be hauled aboard by his cohorts up on deck. I ascended the ladder, climbed over the rail, and never looked baaack."

"So you can't say for certain whether Jorge Aguilar made it aboard the *Eva B.* or not, right? He could have slipped and fallen between the ladder and the ship, correct?"

"That's right."

"Was your pilot boat captain Parker Alley on that trip?" I asked, knowing that it had to have been.

"Yes indeed, it waaaaaaas. Good old Parker. Any luck recovering his body?"

"Not yet. Do you recall who the other crew members were on the deck of the ship when Jorge left? I need to speak with someone who could say he saw him actually get aboard the *Eva B.*"

"These guys aaaall look alike to me. I can't tell one from another."

"Okay. May I have some time with your crew, Captain?" I asked.

I explained to the captain what I needed and he asked his second mate to assemble the eight members of the ship's crew, including the cook, in their mess area. I waited on the bridge for the mate to return and show me the way. The radio was noisy with tugboat traffic, mostly from the two hooked up to the *Asprella*—one towing from the bow and the other secured to her hip—which were making preparations to let the ship go. The captain warned me that the pilot boat would be alongside in about twenty minutes. I was thinking that twenty minutes would probably be long enough for me to ask a few questions. "Only one problem," interjected Willard Kelley. "They don't speak English." I assured Willard that I was comfortable with Spanish, which seemed to annoy him slightly.

Eight men sat at a long galley table and rubbed their eyes in sleepiness. My request had clearly required waking most of them. *"Discúlpenme por interrumpir su descanso. Necesito su ayuda. Tengo que hacerles unas preguntas muy importantes."* I apologized for interrupting their sleep, emphasizing the importance of my visit and my need for their help. I didn't feel as though I had anyone's attention. They looked bored and suspicious; I realized they probably thought I was from immigration and was there to cause trouble, but they had probably been questioned by immigration many times in the past and had all their papers in good order. *"Encontraron muerto a su compañero Jorge Aguilar."* I dropped the bomb regarding their shipmate.

A group gasp and looks of shock assured me that they indeed comprehended what I had said and were now interested in helping. I knew full well that he was probably one of their good friends and I hated giving them the news so abruptly. But time was short. *"¿Cómo? ¡No puede ser!,"* cried a young man in disbelief. There were a few tears and many of the men crossed themselves and mumbled prayers. I told the men that I was aware of the fact that Jorge Aguilar had intended to go home to see his sick wife, and asked who was on deck duty the night he was to start his trip home aboard the *Eva B.*

Two hands shot up instantly. *"Yo era el que estaba de guardia."* One of the hand-raisers said he was one of two crew members on watch that night. The other said he was the second man on watch.

"¿Alguno de ustedes vio cuando abordó el Eva B.*?"* I asked if either man had actually seen Jorge get aboard the small boat. Both men confirmed that they had indeed seen Jorge safely aboard the *Eva B.*

"¿Saben si Jorge andaba metido en líos? ¿O si estaba amenazado?" I asked if the men were aware of any trouble that Jorge might have been in and if they knew of anyone who would want to kill him. Eight heads shook emphatic negatives and the men all frowned in greater shock when they understood that Jorge's death might not have been

an accident. I followed up with questions about Jorge's mental state and asked if he might have been suicidal. *"¿No estaría deprimido? ¿No se habrá suicidado?"* More head shaking and sour looks were accompanied by one voice that stated the opinion that no, Jorge was not sad. He was going home to see his children, who made him very happy.

"Pero que Jorge supiera que su esposa estaba grave podía tenerlo deprimido, ¿no?" I reminded the group that Jorge's wife was very sick, and insisted that this would naturally be a cause of great sadness.

"El suicidio es un pecado mortal." The retort from one of the men that suicide was a mortal sin was irrefutable. Just then the second mate returned and announced that the pilot boat was approaching. This was my exit cue unless I wanted to visit Central America, which I did not. I thanked the group, wished them safe passage, and followed the mate out onto the deck. Two of the crew members came along; it was their turn to oversee the transfer. The mate said goodbye and disappeared up to the bridge, where I assumed he had more important duties to perform.

Willard Kelley leaned against the rail unsteadily. He looked as though his hard night was catching up with him. I was sure he was bound for a terrific hangover once he came out of his drunken stupor. The wind had picked up to a brisk twenty knots or so. The ship was not bothered in the least by the chop, but the running lights of the pilot boat bobbed up and down spasmodically. I was nervous about Kelley making it down the side of the ship and onto the deck of the lobster boat in his present state. The ladder was made of rope and was swinging fore and aft. I assumed that the fisherman captaining the small boat was relatively new to this task, and hoped he had superb boat-handling skills. The ship held course and sped directly into the wind while the lobster boat closed the gap between the two vessels. When the small boat was almost against the *Asprella*'s hull, Willard said, "Wait until I am on the bottom rung before you come dooooown and don't dally."

One of the crew members took Willard's bag and asked for mine, which I gladly handed over. He placed both bags on a hook tied to a coil of rope and lowered it over the side and into the waiting arms of the lobster boat's stern man as Kelley hoisted himself over the rail and onto the ladder. I watched as Kelley made his way down. He hesitated. The ladder was swinging rather violently, with his weight enhancing the pendulum effect. The crew members motioned for me to get moving. I slipped a leg over the rail and placed a foot on the first rung of the ladder. Once I had turned around facing the ship and had both hands solidly around rope, I was quite comfortable even with the swinging motion. I started down the ladder, and waited a few rungs above Kelley for him to make the leap aboard the boat. He seemed to take forever. He was waiting for the perfect opportunity, which might not come, I thought. Finally, he released his grip and fell into the boat, knocking the captain away from the wheel.

I watched anxiously as the two men untangled themselves. With nobody at the wheel, the lobster boat had now peeled away from the *Asprella*'s hull, leaving me dangling over the open ocean. The boat drove away, and then started to circle back to make a fresh landing. The waves had increased, making maneuvers more difficult. I wondered whether I should remain here or go back aboard the ship and wait for the lobster boat to come back alongside. There was some shouting between the lobster boat's captain, the stern man, and Kelley. They seemed a bit frantic, which did nothing for my confidence. They didn't seem to be making much headway. I looked up to the top of the ladder for some advice from the crew. The deck lights were very bright, nearly blinding me. To my horror, I could see the blade of a knife sawing one side of the ladder. *Pop*—it parted. I was now hanging by a virtual thread on a ladder that was heaving back and forth with some velocity. I clung to the ladder for my life. Climbing back aboard was no longer an option. Going overboard in the dark from a steaming ship was certain death. The small boat was coming closer ever so slowly. The knife was working feverishly against the last strand of the rope that held the ladder to the ship. I was all about gut reactions now. I pulled my gun from its holster and took aim just above the knife, where I assumed a head must be hidden by the glaring lights.

14

BUT THEN ANOTHER INSTINCT took over and I paused before firing what could easily be a lethal shot. The ship was changing course, raising the bar for the new pilot boat captain to make and maintain contact with the *Asprella*. But still I didn't fire. I kept my gun and attention fixed on the top of the ladder and prayed that the few strands of hemp remaining would hold. The ship continued to turn. The crew must have radioed the bridge that we were clear. The wind was now blowing directly on my back, pressing me against the hull so that I could no longer see anything above but a black steel wall. And then I realized that I was now dangling right over the lobster boat. I quickly holstered my gun and was snatched like a rag doll from the ladder by the back of my jacket.

I came down hard on my right side directly on and perpendicular to the rail of the lobster boat, which had been at the top of a surge when Willard Kelley grabbed and pulled me to safety. A wave of icy water walloped me full in the face. Kelley and the young stern man helped me off the rail and onto my feet while the captain steered away from the ship. I leaned against the bulkhead, holding my ribs, which I was sure were broken, and watched the *Asprella* slip into darkness while cool saltwater dripped down the back of my neck. "Well, that was what we would call a cluster fuck," said Willard, as he relaxed and exhaled a huge, fully intoxicated breath. "Good job everyone, good jooooob," he continued. I guessed from his reaction that he hadn't seen my gun or the knife while looking up into the bright deck lights. "Nobody's hurt. That's the important thing." I begged to differ, but kept my mouth shut while Willard entertained us with a number of stories of harrowing transfers that made this one seem like child's play.

As Willard regaled the captain and his stern man with tales of blizzards and hurricanes, I suppressed the pain in my rib cage by concentrating on how I would conduct the next leg of this investigation. It wouldn't be possible to interrogate further the crew of the *Asprella,* since they would soon be long gone, and I was certain that the ship would have a crew change before returning to this region a month from now. I couldn't pick the man with the knife out of a lineup of the eight I had seen at the galley table; the lights in my eyes were too bright. He could have been one of the two who were supervising the transfer but he also could have been one of the remaining six. And I had believed the men who claimed to have seen Jorge Aguilar safely aboard the *Eva B.* were being truthful, but now I couldn't be sure.

Every wave that hit the side of the boat jarred my side, sending pain so severe it buckled my knees. When the stern man got busy preparing to grab a mooring in Green Haven Harbor, Willard sidled over to me, placed a heavy arm across my shoulders, and quietly asked if I was okay.

I assured him that I would be fine, explaining that I had reinjured some ribs that I had broken months ago. "Did you learn anything useful from the monkeys about their fellow countryman?" he asked. I shook my head in reply and decided not to take the bait on the "monkey" comment. "Well, I'm not surprised thaaaaaat they were uncooperative. You know, if Aguilar had been found dead in his own country, there would be noooo investigation. Human life isn't held at a premium where they come from."

So Willard was basically telling me that I was wasting my time putting any effort into an attempt to find out what had happened to Jorge. Nice. The stern man was on the bow with a long gaff. I watched him hook the mooring and place the loop over the bit on the bow. He walked back to the cockpit, towing the skiff along like a stubborn leashed dog. The captain shut the boat down for the night. He appeared to be quite frazzled, and I imagined he was questioning his aptitude and stomach for this new job. We all climbed into the skiff; the stern man then started the outboard motor with one easy pull and ferried us ashore to a small dock at the west end of town and far side of the working harbor. Willard offered me a hand out of the skiff, which I accepted. He pulled me onto the dock like I weighed nothing, aggravating the pain in my ribs that had, until then, subsided to a dull ache.

I gladly accepted a ride from Willard, knowing that Cal would disapprove of my traveling with another "creep." But I was a long way from the apartment and beginning to feel the hour that it must be. I directed Wil-

lard along Main Street, up the hill, and into the Vickersons' small parking lot, which was conspicuously empty
in the absence of the Vickersons' Caddy and my Duster. I
would need to get a ride tomorrow from Cal so I could go
retrieve my trusty vehicle from the dock at Bucksport.
"Where's your partner tonight?" Willard asked before I
had a chance to thank him and escape.

"Cal's in bed, I hope."

"Keeping the bed warm for you, is he?"

Jesus, I thought, this guy is repulsive. I would have
allowed him to think that Cal and I shared a bed if Cal
had not been happily married, but I knew how rumors
flew in a small town. "No. He's at his house with his wife.
Thanks for the ride. See you around." I opened the door
and winced in pain.

"Gawd. You really are hurting aren't you? Heeeere,
take this." Willard pulled a bottle of Johnnie Walker from
his bag. "It's great pain medicine." I took the bottle to
avoid any further discussion and thanked him again. Just
before I could slam the door closed, he asked, "Would
you like a little company?"

"No thank you," I said firmly, as I walked away from
the car and into the gift shop, feeling better after I was
inside and out of Willard's sight. His headlights remained
shining on the building until I was safely in my apartment with the door locked behind me. I pulled down the
shades and received a quick honk from the horn as Willard left the parking lot. I suspected he would find some
company with the woman his wife had mistaken me for.
For a second, the hungry feeling in my stomach masked

the hurt that plagued my torso. Although I would not di-
vulge to Audrey the fact that I had been propositioned
tonight, I felt as though I had just proved that I wasn't
nearly as desperate as she made me out to be. In fact, I
was not desperate at all. I just happened to be alone. It's
not a bad thing. I liked being alone. If I repeated that over
and over, it might come true, I thought.

If I ever felt I needed booze to ease pain, physical or
other kinds, I would quit drinking forever, I vowed, as I
put the scotch in a cupboard to enjoy another time. And
that was a vow I would keep. Sometime when I had someone to share it with, I'd have a real treat. Maybe I could
share it with Henry and Alice when they returned on
Friday. The thought was quite depressing. I like being
alone, I repeated. I was surprised to find a bag of coffee
beans in my tote. I stowed them in the cupboard, along
with the bag Lillian had given me. Strange that the crew
would have wanted me to have a gift and then try to kill
me. Obviously, not every member of the crew was involved, I reasoned. Might just be a couple of bad apples.
Or perhaps Willard Kelley had been the target. The answering machine said that I had two messages—two more
reasons to believe that I was not really alone; two people
had been thinking of me. The first was from Lillian Alley. She sounded upset and said she hoped I could be at
her place at ten in the morning. Unless I called and made
other arrangements, she would assume I was coming.
The clock on the microwave oven showed that it was now
one A.M. and certainly too late to call Lillian. The other
message was from Cal. He said that he would be at the

café for coffee at seven A.M. If I needed him to work to-morrow I could find him there. As easy as that, my day was planned. I emptied my pockets in preparation for getting undressed, cleaned up, and into bed. To add to my mood was Parker Alley's suicide note. The guy really was a workaholic, I thought. Who else would scribble their final words on the back of a FedEx shipping re-ceipt? Carl Bagley of Lynn, Massachusetts, had quite a feast coming to him—ten pounds of lobster. I couldn't afford the local lobsters. You had to be a pretty big sport to pay to have ten pounds of them FedExed right to you. I threw my dirty clothes in a heap on the floor.

I nearly scalded myself in the shower, and it felt good. Tension rose from my muscles with the steam and frus-tration spilled down the drain at my feet. I forced all thoughts, formulas, theories, speculations, and fears from my head as I tucked myself into bed. I had only five hours before I would have to be up, and five hours of sound sleep would refresh me enough to have a clear mind with which to begin again. The Guatemalan crew tried to sneak into my consciousness just before I drifted off, but I locked them out to be dealt with tomorrow. Lil-lian must have been upset by something Evan came up with, I thought. Maybe Parker had a secret mistress. That was my last thought before the alarm sounded.

I reached to silence the ringer and was reminded of my ribs. Ouch! Jesus, I thought, I must have really done a number on myself. My standard ten minutes from bed to door was increased to fifteen this morning as I found dressing and brushing my teeth left-handed a bit awkward. Nonetheless, I was in the café before Cal had finished his first cup of tea. "Good morning, everyone," I said to Cal, Marilyn, Marlena, and Audrey. They all smiled friendly greetings as I took the stool between Cal and Marlena.

"What did *you* do last night?" Audrey asked with a playful grin. "You look awful!"

"Thanks," I said, delighted to hear my first voice of the morning, even if it was just Audrey reminding me that I looked like hell. I guess I was pretty lonely. "Coffee, please."

"Ha! It's gonna take more than coffee this morning! Do you even *own* a mirror?" The Old Maids seemed to be enjoying this, as I figured my appearance had taken the heat off them. Cal looked a little embarrassed and squeezed his tea bag relentlessly. "Seriously, just between the"—Audrey looked to my right and then to my left—"five of us. You need a little"—she puckered her lips and I dreaded hearing her opinion of my needs—"TLC."

"Audrey," I said with a smile, "I need caffeine. Please?"

Audrey flipped a mug into the air, caught it by its handle, and poured it full. She then placed it in front of me with gusto as she looked me square in the eye and said, "No. You need more than caffeine. You need the service that only Juan Valdez himself can supply." I started to laugh and immediately grabbed my ribs in pain.

"Are you all right?" Cal asked.

"Yes, I'm fine. I'll be fine. I just slept wrong."

"Slept *wrong*? You mean like a stiff neck?" Audrey blurted out. "You look like you—" The door of the café opened, sparing me Audrey's next shot. "Clyde Leeman! Get out!" Audrey said sternly. "I banished you for a week. Now go. Out, out, out!" I had never been so happy to see Clydie, I thought as Audrey marched from behind the counter to show Clyde the door.

"But it's been a week," Clyde protested.

"Has not."

"Has too."

"Has not." Clyde took a step closer to an empty stool, then hesitated. Audrey took a step toward Clyde and said, "Look at the calendar, Clyde." She pointed at the large month of October on the wall behind the counter. "You see the big 'C L' in the middle of the red circle with the slash through it on last Tuesday?"

"Yes."

"The 'C L' stands for Clyde Leeman. That's you. You're banished until Tuesday according to my records," Audrey stated with some authority.

"Can I get a coffee to go?"

"Sure. Pull around to our drive-thru window."

"Okay, thanks." And Clyde left, looking somewhat triumphant. We all sat and stared at one another.

When we heard the door of his truck open and close, and the engine start, Audrey looked scared. She ran for the door. "Oh my God. Someone has to stop him! There's no telling where he'll end up! Wait, Clyde! There's no drive-thru!" When Audrey didn't come back

right away I pictured her chasing Clyde's truck down
Main Street.

After a few healthy slugs of coffee, I told Cal I thought
we should get going. We left a couple of bucks on the
counter, wished the ladies a nice day, and left. Audrey
stood on the sidewalk chatting up a very nice-looking
young man. She pretended not to know us, turning her
back slightly. Here was the perfect opportunity to embarrass Audrey! What could I say . . . I made a move in
her general direction and Cal caught my arm. "You'll be
sorry," he whispered. He was right. I changed course
and headed for the dock with Cal.

It was another beautiful day. We would be in Cobble
Harbor by nine thirty, allowing me a full thirty minutes
to walk to Lillian's house, and I knew that I would need
them, as I wasn't moving as quickly as usual. Once we
were under way, Cal lit a cigarette. I wanted to tell him
where I had been last night and what had happened, but
really felt that he would prefer to be left in the dark.
"So, what happened to your ribs?" he asked. I wondered if he was curious, or was just being thoughtful.

"Do you really want to know?"

"I wouldn't have asked if I didn't." So I told Cal the
whole story—all but the knife part. And I left out the
scene where Willard was hitting on me and asking
whether Cal and I were an item. I didn't mention the
fact that I had accepted a bottle of scotch either. Come
to think of it, I wasn't all that forthcoming. However, I
did answer his question honestly by explaining exactly
how I had smashed my ribs, and I did mention that I

needed Cal's help in rescuing my car from the lot in Bucksport. Cal finished his cigarette. I finished my story. And we were at the dock in Cobble Harbor.

"Same time, same station?" I asked Cal, suggesting we again meet back at the *Sea Pigeon* at three.

"Good" was all he said as he watched me walk away toward the rows of parked pickups. I couldn't resist searching the lot for Parker Alley's truck, the one that George Paul had borrowed some time after it had been orphaned. When I found the truck, I also found the Passamaquoddy's tribal chief sitting proudly behind the wheel. I smiled and nodded. George Paul waved. What the hell, I might as well go right up to the truck and say hello. There was no sense having him waste fuel following me when I could just tell him where I was going. Maybe he would finally tell me why he was so interested in my investigation.

I approached his open window and said, "Hi." He put the book he was reading on the dashboard and complimented the weather. I couldn't help but notice the cover of the book. It was *Unfinished Voyages,* the same book that Dane Stevens had been reading aboard *Quest.* It was clearly a popular volume. I vowed to check it out of the library in Green Haven, if it was still on the shelves and not already circulating.

"Are you heading to Lillian's again today?" he asked.

"Yes. Are you going to follow me again today?"

"No. I can't. I'm waiting for my ship to come in," George Paul said quite seriously, and stared out at the horizon.

"Okay. Well, I guess I'll see you later." I backed away from the window and headed toward the road. Maybe everyone was right about this guy. Maybe he was a nut and kind of creepy. I expected to see George Paul's name on the enemy list that I hoped Evan had delivered to Lillian. I wondered if George Paul had made the top ten. It was likely, I thought, that the list would be quite lengthy. When there are no immediate suspects or archenemies, this kind of list usually becomes so voluminous that anyone who ever looked at the victim sideways finds him- or herself on it. Enemy lists rarely produce successful results, but often lead to clues that do. I hoped this would be the case today. Otherwise, I would have to throw in the towel on the murder and the disappearance until more evidence surfaced—which could be never. In the past, I had a track record to brag about. Cases I was assigned didn't hang around long enough to get cold. This thought bolstered my flagging confidence.

Lillian stood behind the screen door. But something was different today. She flung open the screen and jerked her head toward the interior, commanding me to follow her without speaking. She walked with a heavy step and had lost that ethereal grace that had so impressed me before. Rather than caressing Oscar, the marble seal, she smacked him solidly on the back and kept right on walking. I entered the kitchen behind her and saw that the counters and table were buried in paper. There were folders, notebooks, reports, and hundreds of loose pages. Lillian placed her hands on her hips and said, "It's gone.

All of our money is gone. Whoever killed my husband has robbed us blind."

It was quite a stunning reversal. And I've almost never seen a human being so changed in a day. She looked older, sadder, and defeated. "Okay," I said, hoping that my calm manner would in some way reassure her. "Let's go over everything. This is going to take a while. Maybe you should put on a pot of coffee." I rolled up my sleeves and got started on the piles of paper in front of me, checking all the recent activity against previous statements. First I organized everything into categories. Then I began going through the stacks with a calculator. Numbers are not my thing, so I had to do a lot of rechecking and recalculating. It seemed that I had been there forever and had barely peeled the first layer. I suggested that Lillian call her accountant or financial adviser to help, and she said she had done that. But she begged me to see if there was anything I could learn about the crime. And I knew that I might get some clues or helpful information from the statements and that she would be more likely to be forthcoming if I had her alone. "So, did Evan ever come up with that list?"

"Oh yes. It's useless. It's right here somewhere. I'll find it for you. He didn't leave anybody out." I told her that I figured that might happen and that I would still like to see the list. She searched a little longer and finally found it. There must have been fifty names on it. The next phase could take months, I thought. Lillian began crying. Not a soft, ladylike weeping as she had done yesterday, but a real heart-wrenching bawl. "Now I have no family and no money. How could someone do such a thing? I'll have to sell this house. You'll find the murderer, won't you?"

"Lillian, have you forgotten about the suicide note?" I tried to be as gentle as possible in reminding Lillian of this.

"They could have forced him to write it. They might have threatened to kill *me*. Parker would lay down his life for me." This sentiment brought on a fresh batch of tears. And then there was a knock on the door, followed by a man's voice calling Lillian. She wiped the tears away and yelled to the man to come in. "That's Evan. I asked him to come over. God, I need him to sell the *Eva B.* quickly." Evan entered, shook my hand, and thanked me for helping Lillian. He said that he was willing to assist in any way that he could. I thought he would need to start by coming clean about the events surrounding his brother's disappearance. I had a hunch, and pieces were falling into place. While Lillian informed her brother-in-law of the shocking news that all of Parker's money had been stolen, and discussed what should be sold and when, I excused myself to make a phone call. I had a little research project for Sheila at the Sheriff's Department.

Sheila promised to call back in ten minutes with information. I returned to the kitchen, where Evan seemed to be processing all the recent developments. He tried to offer Lillian hope that the money could be recovered;

he was sure that the banks and institutions must be partly to blame. "And what about Parker's life insurance?" Evan asked. "When can Lillian collect that?"

"With a suicide note and no body, it's tough. Your brother had just doubled the payout of the policy. I wouldn't count on anything from the insurance company," I said.

"We'll have to sell everything," Lillian cried. "Parker worked so hard to provide for us. This is so unfair. All of his time and effort, his entire life, for nothing."

My phone rang, interrupting Lillian. Sheila confirmed what I had suspected. I thanked her, and she again expressed her pleasure in helping and told me she was eager to assist in the future. Now, how best to relay what I had to tell Lillian? I decided that being fairly blunt probably was the best course. "Lillian, I know that you are very upset, which I fully understand, and that all you see in all of this paper are the zeros at the bottom of the columns. But if you look at the dates of the final transactions, everything was liquidated prior to Parker's disappearance." This news was met with blank stares from both Lillian and Evan. "And that call was from the Sheriff's Department. Someone traveled by bus and airplane using tickets purchased for Jorge Aguilar—that's the name of the body you were asked to ID." Evan sat down, held his head in his hands, and closed his eyes. "I believe that your husband drained your accounts, staged his own death, and disappeared using the tickets and identity of Jorge Aguilar."

Lillian appeared to be stunned. I couldn't tell whether she understood what I had said. Evan opened his eyes, took a deep breath, and said, "I'm so sorry. I guess it's time for the truth. I have been struggling with this for days. I haven't slept a wink, and neither has my son." Finally, I thought, Evan is going to fill in some of the blanks. And he did. He confessed that his brother had come alongside, boat to boat, the morning of the disappearance. Parker had pleaded with Evan to take him ashore to an abandoned dock where no one would see them. Parker had said that he was in trouble and that he was afraid for his life, but didn't say why. He said that he needed to go away while things cooled down, and planned eventually to call Lillian so she wouldn't be distraught over his fake suicide. Evan claimed not to know anything more, and I believed him. "Lillian, I am sorry. I have to go find Little Ev and let him know that I've come forward with the truth. The lie has been killing him." And then for me, he added, "He's very fond of his Aunt Lillian. Oh, and that's why I was so adamant that no one look for him, why I said that I was sure he was dead when we met at sea that first day. I feel terrible for all the trouble I've caused." With this, Evan left.

The slamming of the screen door behind Evan was like the snapping of a hypnotist's fingers, waking Lillian from a deep trance. "But why?" She believed that I knew; in fact, I didn't. But I had a theory.

"I don't know, Lillian. Sadly, people do things like this for many reasons. We may never learn why your husband skipped out. Some sort of trouble he couldn't get out of without making it appear as though he had died? The death of your son could have sent him over the edge."

All of the emotions that Lillian had conveyed up until then—grief, sorrow, remorse, confusion—suddenly morphed into blind rage. She stood and pushed the stacks of paper from the counters and table onto the floor where she stomped on them. "He hated Jason! That bastard! He humiliated and ridiculed his own flesh and blood! And he beat him. He thought Jason was weak and not enough of a man, not good enough in sports, not strong enough. No wonder my sweet baby used drugs. He needed to escape the abuse of his father. You have to track him down. I'll kill him!" I had neither the nerve nor the heart to explain to Lillian that this case was now beyond my jurisdiction. If Parker had flown to Guatemala, the feds would have to pick up his scent. I had reached the end of the road in my search for the missing fisherman.

But now I knew why Jason hated his father; it was, sadly, because his father hated him.

15

THE THING I MOST APPRECIATED about Cal was his willingness and ability to listen. He seldom interrupted me and never broke my train of thought. He just listened. He didn't make facial expressions to influence the next word to come from my mouth, nor did he ever appear uninterested or bored. He just plain listened. Cal kept his opinions to himself, except when I asked or was way off base—like I had been with the red paint. By the time we arrived back in Green Haven from Cobble Harbor, I had said all that I could, and Cal had probably heard more than enough. It had been a long week, and I was pretty well exhausted.

So the Parker Alley case had reached a conclusion. Any resident of Cobble Harbor still waiting for a body to wash ashore could relax. Lillian was broke, but she had some closure. I would hand everything to the state police; I assumed they would in turn bring in the feds to locate and extradite Parker Alley on charges including murder one. The only thing that remained a mystery was the why, and I now had more than a hunch on which to follow up. Not today though. It was five in the afternoon, and I was tapped out. Cal and I parted company in our usual manner, he in his truck and me on foot. Cal agreed to call me after he had a chance to speak with his wife about tomorrow's schedule, and hoped to get me to Bucksport for the Duster. I assured him that I was in no particular rush to rescue my car, and might need a day or two to catch up on the insurance work I had neglected, not to mention needing time to sleep and rest my ribs.

I might be mistaken for a regular Mainer tonight, I thought as I crawled up the hill to my place. An early dinner and bed before the street lamps came on sounded extremely appealing. I knew from past experience that my ribs would bother me for some time to come. But there was no reason to see a doctor. I could tolerate the pain. I had before. However, I did almost give myself a reason to seek medical help when I tripped on the bottom step of the stairs to my apartment. I'm sort of clumsy when I'm tired. I caught my balance, though, so didn't do any damage to my already-injured frame.

A big red "2" was flashing on my answering machine again. I figured I was due to hear from Mr. Dubois about the boat surveys I hadn't done. Preferring to hear his reprimand now and not spoil a fresh day tomorrow, I pushed PLAY. "Hi, Janie, dear. It's Mrs. V calling. We're having the most wonderful time. And the mussels we've had! Henry isn't much good after dark . . . driving that is. So we are staying in Ellsworth tonight and will see you in the morning. Bye, dear." That was thoughtful. Gee, it must be Friday already, I realized.

The second message was from none other than the handsome captain, Dane Stevens. I was delighted to hear his voice. He said that Quasar and he had completed

their work and were not feeling particularly welcome in
Cobble Harbor, so they were making landfall in Green
Haven instead. They hoped that I could join them for
dinner and return the sleeping bag. They knew of only
one place to eat—the café—and would be there around
six, and were looking forward to seeing me. Wow. Dinner out, even at the café, would be nice. And a chance to
see Dane Stevens, and even Quasar, was nice, too. Friday
night is all-you-can-eat fish night. Great! Oh my God! I
didn't have much time to get myself presentable. After
Audrey's comments this morning, I realized that fifteen
minutes hadn't quite done the trick.

I hopped in and out of the shower and began the
Holy Grail–like search for something decent to wear. By
the time I figured out that I wasn't happy with anything
I owned, I had emptied the contents of my bureau draw-
ers and my closet onto the bed. Digging through the sad
pile, I found the lesser of all evils in a newish pair of
jeans and a light blue blouse that had somehow lived its
life without obtaining a coffee stain. I tied a black sweater
around my shoulders the way I had seen sailboaters do.
Slipping into a pair of black flats, I checked myself in the
mirror, knowing that I had to go with whatever the end
result was, as I had no time to change. Not bad. I pulled
the down-filled sleeping bag from under my bed, rolled
it into a ball, and headed out. This was not an official
date, I reminded myself, more of a meeting to return a
sleeping bag.

When I entered the café, my first thought was to give
thanks to Cal for not allowing me to humiliate Audrey

this morning while she was with the young suitor. I was well aware of her propensity for payback. As expected, Audrey, who works every shift of every day, was front and center as I closed the door behind me. She gave me a puzzled look and said, "Hey, I know the service is slow. But come on! A sleeping bag?"

"Hi, Aud." I chose the more familiar nickname, hoping to stay in her good graces tonight. I held the bag out. "I'm returning it to a friend."

"You have a friend?" She sounded rather skeptical. I saw the men seated behind her at a table for four, and waved a hello.

"Yes, there he is." I nodded toward the table.

"The one with the glasses, right?"

"No. The other one." I didn't consider this a lie, as Dane Stevens was my friend, sort of. And this *was* his sleeping bag.

I was sure Audrey was going to ask if I was kidding, but she surprised me with "You vixen!"

"Look, Aud, I would really appreciate it if you—"

"Don't worry." She cut me off before I begged her not to embarrass me. "I won't say a thing. Who do I look like, the Grinch? I wouldn't do *anything* to jeopardize this annual event for you." Fortunately an order was up in the kitchen. Audrey sauntered off, allowing me to join Dane and Quasar at their table.

They both got to their feet to greet me with light, one-armed hugs. We sat and were immediately engaged in conversation; three people off duty and off the record. I gave the men a brief summary of what had happened since they had left me with the corpse in Southwest Harbor. "We couldn't believe it when you left the message saying that it wasn't the right guy," said Quasar. "Unbelievable. Who would have believed it was not the right guy? After that, we were a little trigger-happy. I'll bet we launched the net a dozen times thinking we had another body. We were sure anxious after that news. I still can't believe it was the wrong guy. Weren't we trigger-happy, Dane?"

"And every time we hauled the net back aboard, we were relieved that we didn't have another body," Dane Stevens chimed in. Audrey appeared with a pitcher of water, filled our glasses, and asked if we were ready to order. We all decided on the fish and chips. When she moved to the next table, I breathed again, and Dane continued. "So who was the dead guy?"

I ran around that loop of the story in record time, answering the question, but not in much detail, since I didn't think the part about being aboard the *Asprella* put me in the best light. Waving a gun and breaking ribs are not the most flattering images to share with someone you hope is finding you attractive. "On to nicer topics! Your job for the oyster farm is complete. Congratulations! Will you be getting the bonus?" I asked.

The men shared an awkward moment, making and breaking eye contact. They seemed to be deciding how to answer and who would do the talking. I was ready to change the subject when Audrey saved us all with our meals. She left again quickly. We all got very busy passing tartar sauce, ketchup, and salt. I was not amused with

Audrey's artwork. My fish had been cut and arranged to form a perfect heart in the center of my plate, and a few fries had been placed to make an arrow that pierced the heart, Cupid style. My eyes darted to Quasar's and Dane's dinners. I was glad to see that the fish on their plates hadn't been arranged in any special way. I ate mine quickly, partly because I was famished and partly to destroy the creation of my immature friend. My question about the men's work had absolutely deflated the buoyant atmosphere we had enjoyed before I asked it. Now we were quiet, and I couldn't think of anything to say.

Quasar cracked first. "Let's just tell her, Dane. It's not a secret anymore." My first thought was that they were getting ready to come out of the closet. "It will be in the paper tomorrow. We have good news," Quasar said to me. By the time Dane smiled and agreed that there was no reason for secrets anymore, I was totally intrigued. They started with an apology for not telling me sooner, but added that they just couldn't. Now the men were excited and telling all, interrupting each other to avoid missing any details. It seemed that the "bonus" the men had been pushing for was sunken treasure. As bizarre as that sounded, by the time they had finished, it made perfect sense to me.

In the late 1700s, the ships that comprised the Northeast fleet were busy exporting rum and fish to Africa and bringing home gold and ivory. Although importing slaves had been banned in 1788, some ships still engaged in that awful trade. The Embargo Act of 1807 closed all shipping from the Northeast; the result was a huge increase in

smuggling and piracy. Sometime before the War of
1812—the dates were sketchy—a fully loaded schooner,
the *Abigail,* went down in Cobscook Bay. Because trad-
ing had been made illegal, there was no paperwork, only
rumors of what had gone down with the ship. Dane and
Quasar had researched and found a journal kept by a
member of the *Abigail*'s crew that verified a cache of gold
and gave a detailed description of the land he had swum
to nearby. When *Quest* was hired to do a survey for the
oyster farm, Dane and Quasar had the perfect opportunity to chase a dream.

    The men confided that George Paul shared the same
knowledge; his information was passed down from early
generations of native Maine Indians who had hosted the
shipwrecked crew until they were rescued by another
schooner. George Paul had no resources to attempt to
recover the gold. So he had been working to get legisla-
tion passed to declare the offshore site the property of his
people, which would have barred aquaculture and everything else, and would have given him time to raise money
for a search for the treasure. Dane and Quasar knew that
George Paul had sabotaged their deck equipment and
that he had tried to run *Quest* onto the rocks to delay
their find and subsequent claim to salvage rights. That
explained a lot, I thought, including the book on shipwrecks I had seen both Dane and George Paul reading. It
also explained why George Paul had been following me
and had tried to scare me a bit when he used the truck to
try to push me off the road; he had seen me spending

time with Dane and Quasar and knew that my job as deputy gave them a certain amount of protection.

But I was pleased to hear that Dane and Quasar had no hard feelings toward George Paul and that, in fact, they were going to give the lion's share of the haul to establish a local Native American cultural center and also a fund for sustainable economic development. Their interest was far more in history than in getting rich. And I was also pleased to discover that I had no hard feelings toward George Paul either. I don't think he had it in him to hurt me or them.

We'd finished dessert and coffee, and I was tired. Dane and Quasar would be working out of Green Haven for the next month or so, which I was very pleased to learn. There would be ample opportunity to get to know Dane Stevens better. We planned to meet for coffee in the morning, and I excused myself after being forbidden to contribute to the dinner bill. The men stayed behind for another cup of coffee when I turned down their offer to walk me home, and I escaped unscathed while Audrey was in the kitchen, though I assumed I would be in for a fair bit of teasing over breakfast.

I admonished myself as soon as I realized that I had left my apartment unlocked. Was I that tired, or had I been foolishly fuzzy-headed with the prospect of dinner with Dane Stevens? Either way, it wouldn't happen again, I vowed, as I closed the door behind me and reached for the lights. A hand covered my mouth and jerked me close to a warm body. The pain in my side crippled me, and I

felt faint. I was never totally out, but I was woozy enough
from the shock of the pain that I was unable to put up a
fight. Before I knew it, I was strong-armed into a chair
and duct taped so that I couldn't move. As I gathered my
wits, I knew I needed to remain calm. The shadow of a
large figure moved slowly around the kitchen. Screaming
would be of no use. The Vickersons were in Ellsworth
and no one else lived within earshot.

The small table lamp was switched on, illuminating
the face of the man who stood over it. Willard Kelley
glared at me. I saw my gun under the lamp beside the
phone. I hadn't locked it up, something I never forget to
do. I was mad at myself for that. Willard paced back and
forth on the linoleum a few times, never taking his eyes
from mine. He checked cupboards until he found the
unopened bottle of Johnnie Walker, pulled the other
chair over, and sat facing me. He was jittery, but I'm
guessing he thought the whiskey would smooth the shaking in his hands. He drank directly from the bottle, and
the alcohol loosened his tongue. "Deputy Bunker has
beeeeen very busy."

"What do you want?" I asked.

"Information."

"There are easier and more lawful ways to get information," I suggested. "Could you loosen the tape on my
wrists? My ribs are killing me." I tried to establish a bit
of rapport with my captor and wanted to see if I could
get him to empathize a bit with me.

"When I'm done with you, you won't beeeeee feeling
a thing." Now Willard teetered in the chair a bit and

slurred his speech. The booze had already had an effect. He must have been pretty drunk already. This was not good. Drunk people act crazy. The telephone rang. "Who might thaaaat be?" He reached across to the end table and started hitting buttons on the answering machine to silence the ringing, but had no luck. The ringing persisted.

"If I don't answer, someone might get worried and come to check on me." Willard grabbed the phone, held the receiver to my ear, and aimed my gun at the other side of my head as a reminder.

"Hello," I said as normally as I could, knowing that a drunk had a loaded gun pressed to my temple. It was Cal. He was calling to tell me that Betty wanted to do some shopping tomorrow and that they would be happy to take me to Bucksport to pick up the Duster since they had some errands to run in that area. "Great, Cal. I'll treat you both to a really expensive lunch."

"Betty isn't crazy about fast food," Cal teased.

"I'm not talking McDonald's. I'm talking lobster. A great bottle of wine. My treat. Sky's the limit, pal. Good night." As I hoped, Kelley put the gun down when he placed the phone back on the table.

"I want to know what you know, and whoooo else knows it," Willard said.

"Well, I have everything figured out—including your involvement. And I've already told the whole thing to the sheriff." I figured my best chance of escape lay in convincing him that his cover was already blown and he would be caught no matter what, but be in much worse shape if he harmed me before he was caught. I hoped he would buy it. So I continued, "Obviously, part or all of the *Asprella*'s crew were bringing Parker Alley heroin packed in bags of coffee beans, and he was distributing it around the region stashed inside the freezer packs he FedExed with his lobster. No dog can sniff heroin when it's masked by two heavy scents like coffee and lobster. When Alley's kid died from an overdose, he got jumpy and started preparing his exit strategy. He was worried local law enforcement might start snooping around his home. Someone—I assume the kingpin of the heroin gang—also got nervous. Maybe the gang leader figured that Parker was skimming heroin from the shipments and selling it locally. So the gang leader sent Jorge Aguilar to kill him. The sick wife was a sham to set Jorge aboard the *Eva B.* Parker was tipped off, though—I assume by you—and he killed Aguilar the second he got off the big ship and onto the lobster boat. Parker'd already cashed out all of his savings and was prepared to stage his own death, steal Aguilar's ID, and skip the country using tickets intended for Aguilar.

"How am I doing?" I asked.

"You nailed it," he said. "If he hadn't gotten greedy! Parker double-crossed the connection. Heeee was skimming a little off the top and handing it tooo a local guy. That was the heroin that his poor stupid kid OD'd on. God, heeeee hated that kid. You got to love that the kid got his revenge in death—if the kid hadn't OD'd, then the gang never would have figured out that Parker was selling looocally. Parker and I agreed he would kill Aguilar, but he wasn't supposed to disappear with all the money. Of course, I was supposed to get a cut of the local sale and Parker was saaaaving my cut for me. Now he's double-crossed meeee. He's left meeee holding the bag."

"If the Guatemalans don't find him, the FBI will. Either way, it's bad news for Parker Alley. If you cooperate as a witness, you could get off fairly light and have protection." I thought I was making sense to him as he got up and paced again. Now he was intoxicated to the point of being unsteady. If I could just get my hands free, I was sure that I could get my gun before he did. But my mind didn't stay on that—it drifted to the incident on the boat when I'd cracked my ribs. Who knew how many of the ship's crew were in on the drug dealing? Maybe all of them. And why had Willard saved me from falling into the water? Probably because the new pilot and stern man weren't in on any of this and he had to be seen making an effort to help me. That must have been the argument they had about whether to come back around for me; Willard was probably stalling to give the crew more time to cut the ropes.

My thoughts were interrupted by Willard as he picked up his bag and sat back down. "I don't believe you told anyone. I think you're lying. I think you're theeeee only one who knows."

"Why would I keep something like this to myself? Of course I told my boss."

"I don't thinnnnnk you did. If you had, the whole town would already beeee swarming with cops and feds." He pulled a syringe from his bag. "I think that when the lady chief detective from Miami dies in her apartment from annnnn overdose of heroin, her secret will die with her. Your corpse will be so full of holes, you'll look like a pin cushion. And there's enough dope in that bag of coffee I gaaaave you last night to make you look like the reeeeal dealer around here." He stooped and unplugged the phone line from the jack in the wall.

There was no doubt in my mind now that he would inject me with the heroin. This was not the way I wanted to go. A bead of sweat rolled down the side of my face, tickling my cheek.

Willard placed the phone line around my upper arm and twisted it tight. "My wife will testify that youuuuu called, asking for the ship's schedule. Witnesses can place you at the wharf in Bucksport aaaand aboard the *Asprella*. Don't you think your stories of happening upon the abandoned *Eva B.* and being aboard *Quest* when Jorge was found are a bit tooooo coincidental for anyone to believe?"

Jesus, I thought, I didn't want to die this way. Only Archie would know beyond any doubt that I had been framed. And who would listen to him, his cell mate? No one else knew me well enough to question the scene. Sure, my new acquaintances would be surprised that I used heroin and would tell everyone, "She seemed like such a nice woman." And how would this be explained to my brother, Wally? Just as I felt the needle pierce the skin on my forearm, the door to my apartment burst open, startling Kelley and causing him to stumble backward. I kicked the small table, sending my gun to the floor and out of his reach. I turned to see Cal grab the gun and hold it on Kelley while Dane Stevens and Quasar wrestled the big man to the floor. The syringe had fallen from my arm before Kelley depressed the plunger. The answering machine beeped a warning that time was running out. Kelley had apparently accidentally hit the RECORD button when he was fumbling to shut off the ringer. So he had inadvertently taped his entire confession.

Quasar peeled the duct tape from my wrists and midsection, releasing me from the chair. Thank God for Cal, I thought, who not only got my signal, but stopped by the café for reinforcements. I gave Cal my biggest smile, in spite of the pain in my ribs, to assure him that I was fine. Cal replied, "You owe me and Betty lunch. Lobster. Wine. Sky's the limit, right?"

Author's Note

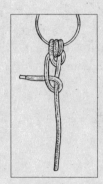 THE FISHERMAN'S BEND is another name for the knot known as the anchor bend. Its most common use is in securing one end of a length of line to the ring at the end of an anchor's shank. It is also handy when making fast a fender to a pipe-style railing. Although most knot-tying sources say "rope," unless you're a cowboy, the correct nautical terminology is "line" or "warp." The fisherman's bend is a tough one to explain in writing, but I'll give it a shot. To tie the knot, pass the bitter end of the line around a post, or through a ring, twice—keeping slack in the second turn. Then pass the bitter end around the standing part of the line and through the slack round turn. Continue around the standing part and tuck the bitter end under itself. If you are dying to tie this knot, I would suggest Googling "Fisherman's Bend," and watching one of the many animations offered. I own a copy of *The Ashley Book of Knots,* and recommend it to knot enthusiasts.

This book was fun to write in that it gave me the opportunity to research some things that have always been of interest to me. There is so much information available on the Internet! The sites that I found useful in learning about Native Americans in Maine were

    www.nativelanguages.org/maine.htm and

    www.nativeamericans.com/penobscot.htm

    The best information on oyster aquaculture was at www.maineaquaculture.org/home

    The sites dedicated to illegal drug use were staggering in number and content. I checked out several of them and found all of them to be eye-opening.

Acknowledgments

THANKS TO ALL who stepped up with clutch performances in the final leg of this voyage; first and foremost, my editor and friend Will Schwalbe. Huge thanks to the dynamic team at the Stuart Krichevsky Literary Agency—Stuart Krichevsky, Shana Cohen, and Kathryne Wick—who were seemingly undaunted by my many requests for help and need of encouragement.

Special thanks to Murray Gray for his answers to my questions about his career and experiences as a ship's pilot in Penobscot Bay. Many thanks to my friend and neighbor Anna Jacobs, for her English to Spanish translations.

Thanks to all of the folks at Hyperion, especially Will Balliett, Brendan Duffy, Jane Comins, Phil Rose, and my very good friend and publicist, Christine Ragasa.

Thanks to my parents, Martha and James Greenlaw, for proofreading and cheering me on.

Thank you, Simon, for your patience.

© Monty Rand

LINDA GREENLAW is the author of the bestsellers *The Hungry Ocean, All Fishermen Are Liars, The Lobster Chronicles, Recipes from a Very Small Island,* and *Slipknot.* Before becoming a writer, she was the captain of a swordboat, the career that earned her a prominent role in Sebastian Junger's *The Perfect Storm* and a portrayal in the subsequent film. She now lives on Isle au Haut, Maine, where she captains a lobster boat.